There Is No Such Place

✣ ✣ ✣

Ignacio Solares

authorHOUSE®

AuthorHouse™
1663 Liberty Drive, Suite 200
Bloomington, IN 47403
www.authorhouse.com
Phone: 1-800-839-8640

First published by AuthorHouse 4/18/2008

ISBN: 978-1-4343-7185-0 (sc)

Library of Congress Control Number: 2008901560

Printed in the United States of America
Bloomington, Indiana

This book is printed on acid-free paper.

Translated into English
by
Timothy G. Compton

from the Spanish original <u>No hay tal lugar</u>

…let us press forward, then, toward our utopia.
Toward utopia? Yes: we need to establish
once again that classic idea.

PEDRO HENRÍQUEZ UREÑA

The Tarahumara people walk insatiably
until they position themselves as another star in the world,
which they sustain with their rituals
so that it can live, so that it can continue.

CARLOS MONTEMAYOR, *The Tarahumaras.*
A People of Stars and Cliffs

WHEN LUCAS CARAVEO, a young Jesuit priest, arrived in the valley of San Sóstenes, in the Tarahumara Mountains, its inhabitants knew it immediately. They didn't see him arrive, but they found out in the same way they learned about any unusual event in that place: their hearts skipped a beat, a unique taste formed in their mouths, or the most common way, they half-closed their eyes and had a simple vision. For the handful of residents of San Sóstenes, reality was a mere excuse for them to see what they really wanted to see. Or what they were unable to stop seeing. When the women would bend down over their fires to blow the ashes off their glowing griddles, they suddenly saw something else. Something entirely different. They could perceive in mere noises the arrival of an unexpected visitor in the sound of water droplets landing on their plants, or in the strident call of a güet, a long-legged bird from that elevated region. The wind that made a racket outside the houses later in the afternoon was also a good stimulus. And the day's final solar rays created all sorts of spectacles on their windowpanes. For that reason, the people of that place could frequently be seen shaking their heads, as if to frighten off a painful vision, or one that bedazzled them. Their pupils would expand as they would listen in the darkness, thus eluding or attracting visions. At night they almost preferred total darkness to the flickering lights of candles, which transfigured things with their yellowish, macabre glow.

And even during the day, when the unfiltered light from outside would enter, the half-lit interiors of their houses became doubly attractive to them, full of apparitions.

Lucas entered the town in the humid afternoon, his feet dragging and eyes fluttering in their sockets like crazed birds. A soft light settled into the air and ground. He walked the clean but unpaved streets, passing by the little white houses with small windows, where, from time to time, luminous eyes flashed. The atmosphere boiled with tepid and contradictory odors. The cold seemed to intensify and condense, causing tree branches to creak.

At a certain moment he had the impression that the streets were rising up against him and that there was a hidden voice crying in each door and window: "Lucas Caraveo, it's Lucas Caraveo!"

LUCAS HAD NO intention of going to that place, buried in the most isolated part of the Tarahumara Mountains, but his superior asked him to do it. In a way, he ordered it. He imposed it as a condition for taking two weeks of leave to go to Chihuahua to visit his family, which he had not seen for two years. His mother had been a little ill, Lucas stated, lowering his eyes as he always did when he spoke with his superior. After hearing him, his superior stood up and opened the window of the sacristy, which introduced a biting, dry wind. The cells of the priests were on the other side of the courtyard, in a reddish structure with a pitched roof, small symmetrical windows and a solid but rusty balcony railing. Next to the residence were the refectory and the workroom, where the Tarahumara children would learn to speak Christian, to spell, and to add. *Wé gara nátame hu.* At the other corner of the courtyard was the kitchen with its tall chimney which spit out curls of smoke, adjacent to the mission's garden.

"Go ahead and go. Visit your family, take care of your mother and get some rest, Father Caraveo. After all, haven't you gone two years without a vacation? But I'd like to ask a favor. You can take care of it on your way. Have you heard of a small town by the name of San Sóstenes? No? Very few people are aware of it, true enough. Rarely does anyone go there because it is located deep in one of the most complicated parts of the mountains, which is saying a lot. There are two ways to get there, but neither is very accessible. It was an important place at the end of the colonial era and at the dawn of the age of Mexican independence, from what I am told, but later it disappeared, went up in smoke, like so many other places up there, as you will see."

The superior was a thin man of a slight build, well shaved. He wore thick glasses with metal frames that hid small but feisty, piercing eyes. He wore a dark suit coat a size too big and by contrast his priestly collar was too tight. He would shake his hand in the air and from time to time his forearm would emerge from the large sleeve like a snake.

"Let me show you something," and from a roughly hewn wooden box he took out a folder which contained what seemed to be a photocopy of a practically illegible text. "Back in the forties, the provincial of our Company became interested in the place, but listen to the message he received from the bishop of Chihuahua: 'In response to your inquiry,… the Bureau of the Interior of the state has informed me that in the valley of San Sóstenes there is not a single inhabitant and that all remaining structures there are in disrepair, among them a few adobe houses and a church. At the current time, the Bureau of the Interior informs me that a lack of resources prevents the funding of any repairs or help for the locale, etc., etc.' How does that strike you, father Caraveo? There's nothing unusual about it, is there? If we were to request a new report, they would undoubtedly answer in exactly the same way. Even though we know that there are indeed people there now, they would give us the same response. They might even copy verbatim the prior correspondence without bothering to go look at the place." The corners of his mouth formed a sarcastic sneer.

In a corner of the room, above the dresser and on a plaster pedestal, there was a bust of Saint Ignatius of Loyola, touched up with brushstrokes of bright colors to the point of caricature, with an open book in his hands which read: "Ad Majorem Dei Gloriam."

"None of this would have any importance," continued the superior; behind his thick lenses his near-sighted eyes darted like fish in a fishbowl, "if it weren't for the fact that about ten years ago, a priest from our Company, Ernesto Ketelsen, left us... and went to live there... with the Tarahumara natives... and the terminally ill. Strange, don't you think? In that place. Actually, Ketelsen was already about to leave the Company; he is the strangest person I have ever met, and although he has an abundance of good qualities, he lacks one of the most important for a Jesuit priest: discipline. First of all he convinced a handful of people from a variety of places (I believe he even took a very sick husband and wife from the state of Sonora) to accompany him to the place and form a type of Ark, at least by the definition of the Italian poet and semi-prophet, Lanza del Vasto. This was to be a rural community that lives righteously in family units on the margins of society and in contrast to it, so to speak. It seems like a sect, but from what I am told, it is not. It specializes in the terminally ill, and they go to San Sóstenes from all over. These are people who need comfort and need to comfort others in similar conditions. What I don't like... is that Ketelsen has become a specialist, from what I hear, in parapsychological experiments. Imagine that! Up in the mountains and among the Tarahumaras! Combine the traditional tesgüinadas --tesgüino drinking celebrations-- and the rutuburi dance with telepathy, hypnosis, and spiritualism and you can only imagine the outcome. It is the most dangerous subject into which a believer can delve. I understand that once in a great while one of them goes down to Creel to buy or sell things, and all of them, I am told, have a very odd manner."

"Very odd?" Lucas became bold enough to ask, accompanied by an involuntary movement of his hands, a trait which surfaced when he was nervous.

"Distant. That's what I am told: they are distant. In addition to their sicknesses, perhaps it comes from an excess of tesgüino. I hope they aren't using peyote," the superior made a contemptuous gesture, waving his hand. "We have plenty of other problems without worrying about a bunch of terminally ill people on whom Ketelsen is performing experiments. But it wouldn't be a bad idea for you to go pay them a visit and then give me a report. It's nothing but personal curiosity, I confess, but since it has to do with an ex-Jesuit priest and the town is in our mountains, I would like to know more."

"Our mountains," Lucas repeated to himself. The superior said it in a tone which made it sound like the mountains really were theirs, the Jesuits.' And in a way they were, since the Jesuits arrived in 1607, despite the frequent rejections and adjustments they had to make from time to time with the Indians and the government. "Being a Jesuit priest in the Tarahumara mountains is being a true Jesuit priest," father Luciano Blanco, one of the founders of the mission, told Fernando Benítez in a famous report. Benítez added: "The Indians are no less than the remains of Paleolithic man, strange beings who, in order to escape Spanish greed, fled to the inaccessible mountains and stayed there in snow and solitude until other white men, attracted by mines, pine forests and scarce arable land, found them. History then repeated itself as these white men hunted them down and took their possessions. When all is said and done, these poor people, stripped of all they possessed, had but one source of help: the Jesuits." It was true, and nevertheless... Lucas remembered the first mass he attended there, soon after arriving in the mission, with enthusiasm (a word with a root meaning something like God-inside) for being a true Jesuit priest bubbling up inside him. At the altar, the officiator and the sacristan quietly conducted the ritual, with mechanical words and gestures, while the Tarahumara assistants scratched their useless rosaries and repeated aloud incomprehensible prayers which had nothing to do with the liturgy. It was as if each Tarahumara were a character in a different pantomime. It was like an orchestra of deaf musicians in which each one played the melody of a different piece, all believing they were obeying the baton of an invisible director. At what moment did that enthusiasm become apathy mixed with the constant crises of anguish which you now suffer, Lucas?

The superior opened an enormous map onto the table. The details of an area 100 kilometers square appeared, hill by hill, stream by stream, town by town, forest by forest. Within a radius of ten kilometers-- "I understand that is a large radius but we don't know where it is, exactly," there were some crosses drawn in red pencil. That was the area of the Valley of San Sóstenes.

"It lies between Norogachic and Samachique, very near Cuacuachique. The problem, as you will see, is that there is no real path. The paved road only goes to here, to Samachique. And then there are the difficulties of crossing these mountains, over here. Be careful of rocks that come loose from the eroding hills. I've seen them when I've been to that area. They are beautiful, covered with moss; they carpet the mountainside, but sometimes they cave in on people, so you are constantly at risk. I've known of several people who have been buried under them. So hire a guide and a horse—you'll need them. Spend a couple of days there, write up a report with all the discretion of which I know you are capable, and then go be with your family to get some rest and take care of your poor sick mother, something you do indeed deserve, father Caraveo."

✤ ✤ ✤

LUCAS'S HEAD WAS sweating under his wide-brimmed felt hat, but out of desperation rather than from heat, because it was actually rather cold. Above him was an ash-colored sky, full of clouds that danced madly back and forth. Sporadic lightning strikes were visible in the distance, but rain never threatened him. In the state of Chihuahua, rain always evaporates exactly one instant before hitting the mountaintops.

The green leaves of the mescal plants looked like burnished copper, and the cloud of dust coming from the slow trot of the horses on which Lucas and his guide rode was brownish-green. The guide was diminutive and plump, his eyes red as if demonic or alcoholic —or demonic alcoholic. He wore a yellow shirt made of heavy fabric and a straw hat with a fringe. In the Tarahumara Mountains, guides are more dangerous than the extreme weather or the rugged terrain, but they are absolutely necessary. Without them, it is entirely impossible to find certain places. Sometimes even with them it is impossible to find some locales and the only certainly is the high risk of being assaulted and beaten, or worse.

The generosity of the Indians, on the other hand, was disarming at times. On one occasion, Lucas dropped a blanket which he had tied to his saddle. Several kilometers later a Tarahumara caught him at a full run, gasping for air, with the blanket in his hands. Lucas tried to pay him, but the Indian said no, indicating his refusal with both his hands and his head, indignant. He hadn't had to track him very far to reach him and acted in pure friendship, not for any personal gain. It was for being a good soul. *We ga pagótame hú.* "Like the ones who walk up there," he pointed to the sky, "who look out for us." The Tarahumara people were like that. But if they ever did accept money, their response was even more disconcerting: "Thank me for taking this, because you have money and I do not."

The longer he studied the eyes of his guide, the less confidence Lucas had in him. His irises were stretched thin and the whites contained lines of blood and spots like tobacco stains on fingers. To Lucas' left a long plateau spread out, brightened by watery sparkles, perhaps coming from a stream hidden among the mescal plants, like an encouraging mirage, he thought. To his right, by contrast, there were high, jagged, serrated rocks, some capped with snow, solid and solitary beneath the sky.

"Over there," said the guide, pointing to his right at the highest peaks, which caused Lucas to shiver unexpectedly.

A gray, cutting, cold wind was blowing. It kicked up some dust which reflected the light. The vegetation on the path they were taking was hostile. Thorns wound around the weeds. But the dust was the worst. At times it would blow away and become almost solid, and you could see it high above looking like dazzling armor. As the day progressed it would start to descend like a dry, fine rain, a very fine powder which wouldn't relent until the next morning, punishing the eyes and stinging the skin. And if the horses decided to quicken their pace it was worse, because it provoked a confrontation between the will of man and the will of the wind, and the loser was always the men's faces, which ended up enveloped in and choked by the cloud of dust, and coated like death masks.

Then, suddenly, just as in dreams in which you go from one setting to another with no particular temporal transition, a river would appear among the tall pines. That was the nature of these mountains. The river, like the mountains themselves, would appear and then disappear, would disperse itself into an infinite number of small streams, then gather itself together in ravines, smoothing rocks, creating granite causeways, lapping against the trunks of pine trees, filling the air with its babbling murmur, its hoarse cry, or its prolonged howl as it fell, like a silver streamer, in the form of a waterfall.

Deep into the night, when they arrived at a bridge, the guide refused to go on.

"I think I made a wrong turn and I want to go back," he announced in his high, parrot-like voice, indicating no shred of doubt.

"How can that be?" asked Lucas, waving his hands in the air.

"It's easy. We shouldn't even look for places like the one you want to visit. I told you that before we even started." Wagging a menacing index finger at Lucas, he repeated: "I told you from the time we left that there was more of a chance that we would get lost than finding that place."

"But I already paid you and I need to go there. Please understand."

"If this is about your damned money, you can have it," and the guide took a wad of bills and threw it onto the ground. "But I'm going back. I don't like this place one bit. It's strange."

"What's strange about it?"

"It just looks odd to me."

"And what can I do about continuing?" asked Lucas in his most conciliatory voice, but adding a tone of mournful complaint at the end.

"Cross this bridge and then pay close attention to the map, that's all," and he clicked his tongue. "Maybe you actually will find the place you're looking for on the other side, who knows?"

The guide pointed out the beginning of a narrow plank of wood: it was a bridge which united the two sides of a deep abyss.

"Alright, I'll cross it."

Lucas got off his horse, secured his knapsack on his back, and with the most resolved attitude he could muster, stepped onto the rickety bridge.

"For Heaven's sake, at least make the sign of the cross!"

"You're right," and Lucas did just that.

The guide watched him make his way across with his arms outstretched for balance, until his swaying figure disappeared into the darkness. His wide-brimmed hat flew off like a kite.

"You're brave, Father, a real man for sure," the guide yelled in an ironic voice. He then gathered up the money he had thrown onto the ground, took the reins of the horses, and returned along the same path.

WHAT THE GUIDE did not see was that, when Lucas was approaching the other side, he nearly lost his balance because of a sudden gust of wind, which placed him in great peril. It really shook him up and sent a shiver down his spine. The babble of water far underneath him in the depths of the abyss beckoned him: "Come down here, Lucas, come here. You don't have to follow the absurd orders of odious superiors. Come and free yourself from your complicated life, your doubts about God, and your priestly vocation so full of contradictions. Come, come down."

He managed to reach the other side, and immediately Lucas realized he was in a "different" place.

Perhaps the sensation was due to fright, a fright he believed he had never felt before, from nearly falling into the abyss. But the truth was that the "other" side to which he had arrived was entirely different--in atmosphere and environment--from the one he left behind.

He was not immediately able to see the terrain clearly, because a type of heavy mist enveloped him and held him tight, choking off his ability to see anything at a distance.

It was not actually a mist, but something similar. Its density impaired his vision, as if volcanic ash were suspended around him.

Or had his fright caused him some sort of breakdown, affecting his sight?

The soil along which he stumbled seemed arid to him and it crackled under his feet as if it were made up of dry leaves or salt crystals. Where was he?

He must have fallen asleep for quite a while because at one point he realized he was seeing the sun round as an orange. He walked for hours (although it is impossible to know how many because he lost all notion of time). He stopped briefly from time to time to study the map and try to eat (although his stomach would accept only water). If a spot started out seeming pleasant to him, it would suddenly turn otherwise, in a strange, incomprehensible way.

He would go to the top of a hill and find himself overlooking the edge of a cliff. Other times he would go down an incline and find himself at the base of an enormous wall no one could climb. He would make his way around it until he found a way out. But a way out to what?

He would fall to the earth exhausted and feel a strange positive sensation. He would take a deep breath, lean his head down toward his chest, listen to the beating of his runaway heart, and feel sorry for himself. What was he doing there, for Heaven's sake, what was he doing there? Or he would throw himself down and place his ear on the ground and think that he was hearing, naturally, a nearby brook. The Tarahumara say that when people stay long enough with their ear to the ground, they can hear it sing. They also say that the state of singing is the highest quality something or someone can attain. People sing, but so do trees, plants, roots, peyote, and *bacánwi*. If people sleep near roots, they can hear the plants sing and move at the same time. Peyote can even sing inside the pouch in which it is being carried. One Tarahumara who used peyote as his pillow was unable to sleep because, he told Lucas, the plant did not stop singing all night.

Lucas raised his head from the earth and no one around him was singing, and nobody was even there. He found just the humming wind and slopes which turned into peaks and valleys formed purely of stone and nothing else. There were deep ravines which intersected with dry causeways--always very dry--and paths on which grey burr-laden thickets were the only rest for weary eyes. He felt dizzy and nauseous; he even tried to vomit, figuring it would make him feel better, but he couldn't, and ended up just arching his back convulsively.

There had to be someplace for him to go. Although his doubts above all else embittered his sense of taste, it also caused a tickling sensation in his hands and throbbed in his temples. For that reason, when he would gather up a bit of strength, he would go on a mad dash, bent over, with his chin on his chest. He would trip, he would slip on the rocks, he would crawl, he would get up and try to get his balance, he would grab onto the trunks of pine trees and scratch up his hands, all the while repeating snippets of a useless prayer, which made its way to nowhere. At one point he was stuck in one spot a long time, cursing, complaining, and making feeble efforts to get up. He finally made progress. He would kneel, then plant his feet one at a time, then pull his hands off the ground and finally take a few steps forward, crouching like a monkey, balancing with the help of both arms to stay upright. Might it have been fear itself which had frozen him? He remembered that the morning Saint Ignatius of Loyola was going to leave Azpeitia to begin his pilgrimage, at the moment he was starting to get dressed, fear overcame him to the point of paralysis--his extremities became so stiff that he could scarcely put on his clothes. Only after enormous efforts did he manage to leave his home, although that same fear followed him like a shadow. After he abandoned the donkey on which he was riding and the knapsack he carried, he was completely and utterly alone in a wild, empty spot, and that was how he regained his faith. Being alone and abandoned had served as an antidote to his fear. Saint Ignatius climbed a mountain, now free of that "evil thing" which he had carried inside his body, and without a drop of doubt, a spiritual force occupied his body with such vigor that he started to shout, sing, and speak out loud to God, whom he was confident he would meet immediately if he died right then. Do you really believe that you would meet your God right now if you were to die here, Lucas?

"EVER SINCE I was a boy I learned to be concerned when I was euphoric, because I always sensed that some kind of punishment was coming, and that it was imminent." Gray peppered the hair of Lorenzo and profound wrinkles on his forehead seemed to open up as he started to speak in the confession group. "I've never been wrong in that way. Just two years ago, I met the woman with whom I live. I fell in love with her the moment I first saw her. We were working in the same building but didn't know each other. One morning we took the same elevator. I sensed that something important would happen to me on that day. I felt it when I got onto the elevator, which started upwards for several floors puffing and groaning. The jerking and shaking of the wood and glass box as it went past each successive floor started to make me nervous (I hate elevators). It suddenly stopped, in a type of hiccup. The elevator door opened and allowed us to see a long, empty hallway, almost dreamlike, at the end of which I saw her coming, running to reach the elevator. I pushed all the buttons, amid complaints and threats, but I managed to delay long enough for her to get in. She thanked me with a slight nod, which was enough. For just a moment, I had her so close that I was able to take in the breeze of her magical aroma. I looked at her out of the corner of my eye and she seemed so beautiful, so different from ordinary people, that I couldn't fathom why other people didn't feel unsettled like I did by her very existence, by the way her heels hit the ground as she took her first steps out of the elevator; nor did their hearts skip a beat when they saw the movement of her skirt as she walked; nor did they fall madly in love with the bounce of her hair, the movement of her hands, or the light in her eyes when she noticed me at her side, asking her desperately for her name, her phone number, and the office where she worked. I left my family, and a month later I was living with her. Since then we haven't been apart for a single moment. I'm not exaggerating when I say that, because I even managed to have her transferred to my office as a secretary, so we would arrive at and leave work together. We would go to bed at the same time, in the morning we would open our eyes at the same time, we would eat in the same place and--please don't laugh--we would eat the same things. In a word, despite the apparent contradiction, two became perfectly one. But as I said, I sensed that such happiness was impossible, terribly impossible, and when we discovered her leukemia, it didn't surprise us. It had to be that way. They say that heaven castigates its chosen ones. The only thing I asked for--one thing and nothing else--was to die with her, at the same time and in the same place. The problem was where. Where we were living, two deaths would have caused too much of a stir, so we had to get away from there. Happily, the treatment went well and she hung on better than we could have guessed. But the moment arrived to prepare for the end. I started to do some research--in many fields, including the field of ethics--and discovered, among other things, that the writer Arthur Koestler founded in the eighties a Society of Voluntary Euthanasia, which is dedicated to lend support to those who decide to shorten their agony. His arguments seem irrefutable to me. They convinced me that adults with a serious or incurable illness should have the legal right to a dignified, painless death, if that is their expressed desire. We should recognize that our species suffers from (along with other obvious flaws) two grave biological disadvantages, which are imposed upon entering and upon leaving this world. Animals give birth painlessly or with a minimum of discomfort. But because of some rarity in evolution, human fetuses are larger than the birth canal and their hazardous passage through it brings a prolonged and painful task for mothers and (presumably) a traumatic experience for newborns. Hence, we need midwives to help us be born. A similar situation exists for our departure. In general, animals--unless they destroy each other or we destroy them--die peacefully, without serious complications. I have not met or read any ethnologist, naturalist, or researcher who described anything to the contrary. The inescapable conclusion: we need midwives, also, to help us be un-born, or at least the assurance that such help is available to us. Euthanasia, like obstetrics, is a natural and human solution to a biological problem. Koestler himself committed suicide in his apartment in London, at the side of his young wife, with whom he was madly in love. Why do mature men such as myself fall madly in love with women who are much younger, and why, in so many cases, are those young women the ones who get sick and die? The Koestlers' maid found them the next day in their apartment, cold and stiff, sitting next to each other, holding hands, with a pitcher of poisoned tea on their table. Even their dog was dead. It was all very British. By contrast, in Mexico City the discovery of our cadavers would have caused a scandal, especially because of the presence of my prior family and the tabloid press. Imagine the photo they would have published of us in the magazine *Alarma.* Where would they have buried us? Who would have attended the burial? I believe, I am convinced, that my current wife and I will continue to be together in the next life--and perhaps in several subsequent lives--and that is why we care so deeply about the days following our deaths. We have been advised in the *Tibetan Book of the Dead* that it takes seven days for the soul to separate from the body. It directs offerings be taken to the dead. At very least, I am pleased to avoid the focus of the media and the shrill complaints of my ex-wife--she always talked to me with a loud voice.

While I was doing research on the situation I learned about this place and, despite the immense difficulty of getting here, we came to die here, content, in your midst. Father Ketelsen has proposed throwing an extraordinary party the day of our funeral, with music and tesgüino alcohol--lots of it. I brought part of my life savings and have arranged to have some colorful decorations garnish the town, as well as a special meal and gifts for everybody. We would like to send out a formal, printed invitation to everyone, but since we don't know the exact day and hour--although we are certain that we are not far from it--some of our friends have offered to spread the word at the proper time. In other words, this won't be a goodbye, but a see you later. May God bless each one of you."

FINALLY, SUDDENLY, PRACTICALLY in the blink of an eye, Lucas arrived in a deep, narrow valley, very green and unexpected, in which the town of San Sóstenes was buried. It did exist. Here and there, intermittently, as if dropped in place at random, he saw little white houses; others were pressed close to each other on the sides of neatly constructed stone streets; sheets of mist stretched out and mingled with the timid smoke which emerged from chimneys. The dome of the church sparkled under a transparent light. The valley stretched upward, losing its color in the distance, until it disappeared and was replaced by muted, arid mountains. Lucas understood why no one ever found it. "This is a mirage," he told himself. He took a path which wound its way through sporadic rectangles of pale wheat and languid stalks of corn.

    Lucas entered into the town in the humid afternoon, his feet dragging and eyes fluttering in their sockets like crazed miniature birds (with the inhabitants of the town sensing that he had arrived even though they had not seen him). It seemed to him that the streets were rising up against him and that there was a hidden voice crying in each door and each window: "Lucas Caraveo, it's Lucas Caraveo!" With a final burst of energy, from a reserve he did not know he possessed, he pressed toward the church: a tall block of stone crowned by embattlements and surrounded by enormous buttresses (the apse was massive). The weather and rain had darkened the stone, covering it with dense lichens and reddish rust. It had to be extremely old, he supposed; one of the first buildings the Jesuits in the region had built. The gate was closed and the outer patio vacant, inhabited only by old pine trees which were bending gently in the wind. Lucas caught hold of the bars on the gate. He unfurled a sudden, dry shout, the start of a bellow which ended abruptly, like a tense chord, and then he lost consciousness. He fell to the ground exhausted, like a marionette whose strings have been cut.

"Are we finally back?"

The tall, portly body of a woman seemed to appear suddenly at his side, as if produced by the final mirage he saw in the mountains. Was it a mirage? He felt her next to him, felt her hand removing the fever from his forehead and cheeks. He sensed a whisper of supplication near his face.

"We are back, here and now, aren't we? Here and now, here and now."

Lucas squinted to study the darkness that surrounded him. Objects vaguely started to emerge: rough walls, a crude wooden cross, a trunk that seemed very old, a lopsided table, clay pots, tree trunks which served as seats. A small fire burned serenely in a corner. He tried to sit up in the bed, but was unable, and gave himself over to the sensation of calm, with that cool hand on his forehead which seemed to bring him back to the world and kept him from any other kind of fall.

"Your name is Lucas, isn't it?"

She said his name in a tenor that Lucas had never heard before-- or perhaps it was just a product of his emotional state--charged with something that went beyond the mere pronunciation of a name, even if it was his own name.

"Yes--Lucas."

"Go ahead. Go ahead and tell all of it immediately."

"Tell what?"

"Everything. Tell all of it. Now. Later it will be too late. Your memory is still fresh."

The woman's hands, her soft voice, her breathing, and the way her fingers ran over his cranium, his forehead, and his eyes--they all filled him with peace and transported him to a hazy past.

"I very nearly fell..."

"Where? Go ahead."

"At the bridge."

"You have to tell all of it. Go on."

"If I do..." he hesitated, then whimpering, with tears slowly moistening his cheeks then disappearing into the incipient beard which was starting to darken his face, "...if I tell the whole story... it will be like living it all over again."

"Precisely. Go ahead and tell me all of it."

Lucas couldn't control his breathing, which swallowed up his words and seemed to carry them ever deeper into his body.

"I can't."

"Then you'll never be free from it. You'll carry that feeling with you the rest of your life. And you'll deserve it. Let go. If you can't face it, I will. Remember the abyss. Isn't that it?"

"How do you know about the abyss?"

"Oh, I know."

"But how?"

"What does that matter? Remember every detail of it. The fall. The babbling of the water below. Actually, it's as if you did actually fall. You did fall."

"Yes, I fell. I fell."

"But you didn't fall and now you are here," her skittish smile, which would appear then vanish, stayed on her lips for a moment. "Go on."

"It was like a dream I had as a child in which I was falling, falling, falling... I kept on falling... I would wake up and it seemed like I was waking up, not from that dream, but from a longer one, much longer, in which I was also falling, falling..."

With his hands knotted together Lucas masked his face.

"And then what happened?"

"It wasn't later. No. It coincided with the moment I was about to fall..., at that instant I felt very vividly, more vividly than ever..., the sensation that at the bottom of that abyss... there wasn't anything. Nothing at all. I looked for His face, but found nothing at all."

He then realized that, while he was speaking, she was kissing his forehead, his cheeks and his eyes, all the while whispering to him tender, sweet, incoherent words, like when we whisper to children and the sound itself, the whispering of a voice soothes them.

WHEN HE HAD calmed down a little (the artery in his neck was no longer pulsing as if about to burst), the woman, who said her name was Susila, took him a cup of gold, steaming tea that smelled like bitter herbs, and a plate of beans and tortillas. Lucas tore a tortilla in half and dipped it into the warm beans to soften it. He started to take tiny bites indicative of someone who can only swallow with great effort. But his palate started to register his sense of taste. When the final piece of tortilla dissolved in his mouth it seemed more delicious to him than an entire banquet. His hand, which he thought he remembered injuring on a rock, had a gash on it which throbbed steadily.

"Drink the tea also," Susila ordered in a tone that contrasted with her prior sweetness. "If you believe that it can heal you, it will. God created plants to cure us if we believe in them."

"What kind of tea is this?" he asked, then took another sip, savoring it, his eyes feeling better.

"It is a mixture of an herb called simonillo, good for the spleen, and another called princess petal, good for sunstroke."

"I'll take the recipe back to the mission."

Susila then told him about the place where he had arrived.

It was made up of just a handful of people--no more than 200--although the number varied greatly from time to time. They were from all over the country, and some even came from other countries. And there were Indians from the mountains nearby. People would appear there just the way he did, suddenly, as if sprouting out of the depths of the earth. In particular the sick and moribund would arrive and would never depart. They needed to be buried there, in the town cemetery, which had run out of space. Sometimes Father Ketelsen was able to cure the inhabitants through hypnosis, bringing them back to life. Others he could not. Father Ketelsen was able to give others, if they so decided, a reason to die in peace. Or a reason to live while they were alive. It depended on the person.

"How do they get here?

"On the train."

"A train comes all the way to town?"

"Of course. The station is just outside of town."

Lucas raised a hand in front of his face as if he were moving the branch of a tree to get a better view. Or perhaps it was more like removing spider webs from a nightmare.

"I can't believe it."

"Go to the station. See it with your own eyes."

The Indians were the more permanent group of people in town--a small group of Tarahumara families. Susila seemed proud of the work they had done with the Tarahumaras. They had helped rescue them from their caves, from neglect, from starvation, from living death. In the outskirts of the town Lucas surely had seen them--as he was coming down the narrow canyon-- the mountainside had burned with the light of their innumerable fires. How could he have missed them? Along the sides of the path, under pine trees, at the entrance to their caves, the crackling flames of fires made ancient figures emerge from the darkness, figures of women with their heads covered, children sleeping on worn mats, old men and young men with prominent cheekbones. You could see them through the smoke of their fires and the steam from their pots in which they were cooking their paltry meals. The mountains were full of these ghost-like figures. Lucas surely had seen them.

They had helped some come down from their caves or from their old stone cabins which were about to collapse, in which they kept fires all winter long which may or may not have kept them warm, but assuredly covered them with smoke to the point of making them unrecognizable, and even more ghostly. Instead of hunger, dirt floors, and leaky roofs, a small group of Tarahumara Indians was now benefiting from healthy, steady food, airtight windows, wooden floors, stoves, antibiotics, brooms and dusters. In addition to teaching them to read, write and work the land, of course.

"It seems incredible that word of this hasn't spread to the surrounding towns."

"That is our one fear. We try not to publicize what happens here very widely. Let those who need to come here come, and no more."

"Those who need to come here?"

"You'll see. People come here because they know that they need to."

"Tell me about Father Ketelsen," asked Lucas, remaining seated on the bed, leaning back on a pillow. She smiled at him with her entire body, leaning forward in her chair, her torso quivering. He smiled in return, noticing the triangle of her neckline as she leaned forward.

"After he left the Jesuits he wandered about the mountains. He said that he was in a state of desperate availability, but it was really just a delay, nothing but a test.

"Of what?"

"Of everything."

"Oh," Lucas drew the corners of his mouth into a grimace which never turned into a smile.

"That's how he described it to us--for the first time his life seemed to be a river of continuous events, with a current which ended up here, where everything took on meaning, had an explanation, and existed for a reason. He became completely convinced that there was a central hub, a unique center, deep in the mountains, in which every situation, even the most discordant ones, could come to be seen as the spokes on a wheel. Something like that. That's what he was seeking.

"That happens a lot to the Jesuits who leave the Company."

"He spent so much time wandering through the mountains that he had a case of sun stroke and went half mad. Imagine that! His devotion and kindness endeared him to the Indians, who adopted him as if he had lived among them his entire life. The children started to include him in their games and even the fiercest of dogs started to allow him into their houses without barking at him, letting him pet them when they had never let anyone pet them before. He spent hours and hours with the sick and moribund, cooling their foreheads and praying for them. Sometimes he would even share their final agonies and hallucinations. They say that about then he started to discover his gifts in seership, and he decided to develop them to benefit the people in this area. He could see what they could see at the moment of death. But deep down he was still the same person. He would still go to the towns down below to drink beer with the *chabochis* and would also spend entire days with the Tarahumaras in their putrid caves. He would teach them to speak and read in Spanish and to pray, but he would always go with them to their parties and drink *tesgüino*. He is quite renowned as a drinker of *tesgüino*--I have seen myself that even when he drinks and drinks he never gets drunk. He would seek out the most difficult and undesirable of situations, like helping older people who had lost the ability to take care of themselves. At night, instead of becoming fatigued like everyone else, he would stay up. He would eat only what was donated to him, and he would always eat so sparingly that he would take part of the food the faithful would leave him and each afternoon he could be seen handing things out to the poorest of the Tarahumara Indians, who were very poor indeed. One day he finally found this place and decided to found a small community. He had read mountains of books on it and wanted to put those ideas into practice. The Indians must have followed him not so much for what he said, but for the conviction he communicated with his voice, which, as you will hear, is enchanting, but at the same time smooth and impersonal. This place has become recognized as one to which a person can go to die in peace, which was really needed, I think you'll agree. It has gained notoriety and now more and more people come to our confession groups.

"Did you say 'confession groups?'"

"That's what we call them. We talk about ourselves, about our lives, about the happiness we've enjoyed or the pains we've endured, but above all else we talk about our imminent deaths. Because one thing is for sure--we are going to die."

"There's no doubt about that."

"There are people who come here just for consolation from loneliness and sadness, even though they have no real physical illness, and then they stay."

"They don't leave?"

"They can if they want, but despite all the people who have come here, no one has ever gone back."

Lucas felt a subtle shiver as he repeated it to himself: "no one has ever gone back."

"What about hypnosis?"

"Ketelsen emphasizes over and over that he is not a witch doctor or a physician, but when it is critical he hypnotizes people to remove an ill from them. Or he takes them to a hypnotic death to allow them to live after the resurrection. Let me assure you that you can't ever be the same person after experiencing resurrection."

"I don't suppose you can."

"During the day, in addition to routine chores, which vary quite a bit, we try to practice concentration, intuition, and communication from a distance. Those all help us to die, but even more importantly, they also help us to live. We try to guess what someone, in some other place, is writing or drawing. Children especially find this entertaining. A lot of the people who come to die bring their children, and they all stay."

"Are there a lot of children?"

"Quite a few. Some of their parents died, but plenty of other families adopt them as their own. I can assure you that in our kind of environment, children don't even resent their parents' absence."

"What about you?"

"What about me?"

She smiled at him across the bed sheets with a smile reminiscent of a flower he had kissed before. Her dark almond-shaped eyes smiled at him, but so did the lines of small, very white teeth, her brown hands clasped on her lap, and the borders of her fitted shawl.

"I am from Durango. I worked in the mission of the Tepehuan Indians, where I became convinced that I had been born to teach and live among children, especially among Indian children, who are the sweetest in the world. I married a teacher there, the director of the Santa María de Ocotán school. My husband had a weakness for theosophy and made me read a pile of books on the subject. He also enjoyed music and played the violin in a way that (to me, at least), seemed unequalled. He died in a highway accident and, perhaps as a consequence of that, a few months later I was diagnosed with uterine cancer," two very white teeth suddenly appeared which momentarily rested on her lower lip. "I had surgery and radiation treatment, but it came back. That is why I came here, to a place where I can die in peace, without fears, and where I can exercise my pedagogical vocation… I think that the only future that can enrich the present is the one that comes from a present that sees itself very clearly, face to face."

"Here and now."

"That's right. Here and now."

"Where might I be able to stay and sleep?"

"Right here. This is for people who come unannounced. A lot of people do come unannounced, let me tell you. The door doesn't have a lock. No door around here locks. We don't use money, so you don't have to pay us anything. Just try to learn the location in case you need to come home alone. Are you feeling okay? If you are, come with me to a session of the confession group--it should be about to begin."

When Lucas went out to the street, he started to feel once again that he was falling… or that the night itself, in its immensity, was weighing down upon him. But he drew a deep breath and endured the feeling of instability. At one point he had to hang on to Susila's arm. He felt that perhaps he was experiencing the final surge of blood to his temples. It seemed to coincide with the pulse of the mountains and the sky, and the borders between time and place were becoming blurred.

What if, when he arrived at the confession group, he were to ask to speak, and should say: "My name is Lucas and I am going to die."

A TUFT OF grey hair floated above Elvia's forehead, and a tiny spark emanated intermittently from her brown eyes, tiny but very much alive.

"This entire time has been, how can I put it, a time of waiting (although I don't know what for), of sterility, and of bewilderment. Everything has been baffling. Everything has had equal, identical proportions, and equivalent meanings. Everything has been stripped of importance and takes place outside of time and life as I have known them. Everything is the same from day to day. I see a gesture repeated, and a distant anticipation (even though, as I told you before, for what I don't know) starts to vibrate outside of me, in the air and in objects which suddenly appear, and transfers into my idle hands. Am I making myself clear? Whether my eyes are open or closed I see the same obstinate image of waiting (for what? I ask myself, for what?), followed by or preceded by the same acid smell, the same foul sense of exhaustion, the same remnant of an interminable shriek which began in darkness who knows how many centuries ago and which I inherited. My daughter used to get very angry with me. She would visit me and I would drag myself across the floor to get to the door. I'm not exaggerating. A medical doctor saw me and diagnosed me with a nervous depression so severe that it could kill me at any moment. He prescribed a handful of medicines that didn't help a bit. My daughter tried to feed me orally, with no success: 'How can you not want to eat anything, Mother? Maybe it's because you spend the whole day lying down. Who could work up an appetite doing that? If you would just get a little exercise. If you would at least get up to open the door for me instead of dragging yourself across the floor like a worm. I'm not asking for the impossible. I just want you to give a little effort. You heard the doctor--you don't have any illness--you're perfectly healthy. I'm not going to hire a nurse to help you--that would be like saying you're right.' So I would ask her: 'Then why can't I move? Look! I can't even hold up a spoon.' And she would say: 'That is what I would like to know, Mom, why you can't move.' And I would explain: 'I've been living alone for seven years, which is quite a few, as you know, since your father died. I had a terrible relationship with him at the end. What a nightmare to live with a man from whom you want to distance yourself. As soon as he died I felt free. I lived as I always wanted to live: peaceful and free from pressures of all kinds. I haven't even pressured you in any way.' 'And then what happened, Mom?' 'And then began the wait for I don't know what,' I answered. 'Bah! The wait for I don't know what!' she repeated, furious. She would leave, slamming the door, or she would start to cry inconsolably on my lap. One day she accused me of breaking up her marriage, which pained me to the core and made me take action. I said to myself: 'Get out of here as soon as you can. Go to where you can wait for what you are waiting for surrounded by people who are waiting for the same thing."

ARRIVING FROM THE clear night outside, the dark interior of the room seemed doubly impenetrable. After several minutes had gone by, Lucas was finally able to make out a group of shadows. The first thing that his greedy eyes took in was thick cigarette smoke, which spiraled upward in the dense, confused atmosphere, barely lit by a kerosene lamp hanging from the ceiling. When the lamp would sway gently he could see cracks that looked like scars on the walls, and spots--dark clouds--that would change forms. In one corner there was a dilapidated niche in which, at the feet of a plaster Virgin with Baby Jesus in her arms, several burning candles were about to finish their existence.

But even if the faces and movements on the edges of the room were dimmed by the darkness, in the middle, directly under the kerosene lamp, blue light magically shaped the feature players of the scene. Those who were going to speak formed a small circle inside another larger circle of participants. The individual who was speaking sat in a chair in the exact center, and very near, to the side, was a diminutive, frail old man, dressed in a faded purple robe with buttons down the front. He wore the sandals of a shepherd. Ketelsen, Lucas told himself, with the sensation that he had seen him before, somewhere, but he didn't know where. He had sparse, grey hair and a matching beard, deathly pale skin, and dark eyes with enormous pupils. His broad forehead and depressions at his temples seemed to suggest that he was a daydreamer. A hook-shaped nose. He would half-close his eyes as if trying to conceal his flaring eyes, the secret passion which consumed him as he listened to what he was hearing. His attitude, and particularly his exaggerated pallor, suggested to Lucas a type of serene coolness, like water in the moonlight. He also thought that underneath that glacial mask a lively fire was burning, like coals glowing under their own ashes.

But perhaps the thing that impressed him the most was Ketelsen's hands. Big-boned, with long fingers like vines and raised, dark blue veins: virtually rivers with branches, tributaries and deltas.

Someone offered Ketelsen a cigarette which he accepted. He held the cigarette with two fingers as someone lit it with a match. He held it tight in his mouth and the first puffs of smoke emerged from his curved nose.

Lucas opened his eyes and ears wide and, controlling his breathing, could hear even the creak of chairs, the monotonous song of the wind coming through the gaps in the windows, the whispering among the attendees, especially among the ones sitting on the perimeter. In general, the people attending the meeting seemed deeply absorbed and effervescent, but also emaciated and pale. Perhaps for that reason every word and every sound surprised Lucas and reverberated through his being, as if his nerves extended beyond his skin, sensing the entire room and picking up its most minute vibrations.

On one of the walls there was a large metal crucifix, the exceptionally twisted torso of which projected its terrible shadow on the back wall.

A man named Miguel started to speak. His elongated face became even thinner as the light of the kerosene lamp would catch it for brief moments. He wore pants that were frayed at the hems, and cowboy boots.

"I want to say… I want to tell you… It happened when I found out about my illness… The day after I found out, in the morning, I opened my eyes and saw that the sun was coming in through the curtains in my bedroom. Sunlight like any other day. At that exact moment I felt a horror that seemed to convulse through my entire body, a kind of rebellion of my body and soul. I lived, simply put, the horror of being ill, of not ever being the same again. And that was it. It was horror that came from recognition, from becoming informed. Why me? Later on, here, when I came and told my story for the first time, which I am repeating now, Father Ketelsen told me that what I had been through was one of the worst experiences a person can have. He read something that expressed my feelings exactly. It was from Dante, I think--Ketelsen nodded his head in agreement--which said more or less that… there is no greater pain… there is no greater pain than to remember happy times during times of sadness. That line alone captured my confused feelings. The sun, that sun, became a symbol for me… It was the sun we see every day, really. The same sun. The sun again. Whether you like the sun or not. The sun will rise at six thirty even though a tumor is growing inside your body. The sun rises on the healthy and on the ill day after day…"

There was a heavy silence, interrupted only by the sound of people shifting their weight on their seats, clearing their throats, and whispering in the shadows.

Ketelsen spoke with his thin voice, sounding almost like a meow.

"Days are like trained birds: they come to the entire world every 24 hours, always from the same corner of the globe, and they envelop us whether we want them to or not into their eternal song, sometimes monotonous and sometimes novel, sometimes sweet and sometimes bitter--it depends on the way you listen to them. Before thanking Miguel, would anyone like to have the floor to comment on what he said?"

A tall, thin woman raised her hand and stood up. "She is a poet from Mérida," Susila told Lucas. "From where?" "From Mérida--she just arrived." She spoke with a rounded mouth and at times she seemed to take on attitudes and movements as sappy as a heart carved on a tree. She unleashed an interminable, insipid lecture, plagued with clichés, about the function of poetry in daily life, especially at key moments of life, and particularly on death's doorstep, where she said she was. Finally she recited two of her own poems--which included numerous repetitions of the word "rainbow." Lucas started to nod off, and his eyes drifted to a dark corner of the ceiling, the darkest spot in the room, which seemed to grow darker as he looked at it. Finally, sweetening even further her gooey voice, the woman fervently asked Ketelsen to comment, pretty please, on what she had just said and recited.

Ketelsen softly clicked his tongue, which revealed, whether he wanted it to or not, his opinion about the poems he had just heard. Susila later told Lucas that she had already recited those poems twice before, Heaven have mercy on us. Finally he said that our problem is that we are unaware of the source of our pain, as Miguel had just said. We see babies cry in their cradles, for example, and we feel desperate because we would like them to tell us where they are hurting to take care of them, to comfort them, to cure them if possible. But cries alone do not reveal the precise source of the pain. The same thing happens to us. We cry but we don't know the location of our pain. Poets have an advantage because they know how to express the location of their pain. Poetry--real poetry--indicates the location of pain. That is why when Dante said that there was no greater pain than to remember happy times during gloomy ones, he was expressing his own private feelings, which in his matchless poetry reflected all of ours.

Ketelsen then thanked Miguel, who returned to his original chair, and asked whose turn it was to speak next.

Lucas thought back to his time of exposure in the mountains, scarcely a few hours earlier. How could it have been real--really real--that he had suffered in that terrible sun, that it prolonged his agony indefinitely, that the clouds didn't move to bring him comfort and that a bird was floating over him for hours without even moving its wings. How could you forget that, Lucas? How will you manage to tell about it?

The words multiplied in the dark room, piling up memories and yearnings.

Before burning out, a flame enlarged around the wick of a candle, and the skittish darkness retreated to the furthest corner of the room.

As time marched on, the participants in the group hardly moved, as if they were playing the game of statues, with frozen gestures, Lucas thought, but always with a latent enthusiasm in their eyes, passionately taking in the final sparks of the night and their common misery.

Finally, his tiny soprano voice contrasting with his fiery eyes, Ketelsen spoke of the penitence necessary to destroy one's own will. He said everyone needs to overcome the poison which causes them to think that they are little gods superior to God. He also spoke of the advantages of having a place like the one where they were meeting, and of the need to protect it, take care of it, and make it holy so that it would not become corrupted. The discussion, although religious and profound, could not be called solemn. It was relaxed, like those pleasant after-dinner chats families have as they gather around their fireplace. He indignantly criticized the hospitals "down there"--and he pointed at the floor--where people died scarcely realizing that they were dying (the worst death possible), plugged in to horrible torture machines that just prolonged their pain. We don't grieve over suffering, he said, but over suffering for no particular purpose. For that reason, people come to resemble their own suffering. Why did human beings lose touch with the dignity and meaning of death? Did they remember the lines by Rilke, which he had recited to them so many times:

"Send us, oh Lord, the death that suits us,

The individual death that is born with us

The one in which each person discovers love, necessity, and meaning."

They had there, in the town, sufficient pain-killers to mitigate pain without depriving people of living their death. Or assistance for those who would like to leave earlier, should they so decide. And much to the astonishment of Lucas, who could do no more than blink his eyes, Ketelsen started to talk about elephants. In all of Africa one does not see, either near roads or in the jungle, a single dead elephant. And you can't say that elephants bury their dead. No, they have secret cemeteries, which they do not even realize exist while they are alive, and that is where old elephants go when they believe it is time for them to die. Without being constrained in any way, they go to the place--which they find by intuition--then they lie down and wait to die. They don't wait until they are immobile. At some moment they simply lift their trunks, bellow a farewell, and off they go to the secret cemetery. In like manner, he explained, they needed to keep this place sacred, like a secret cemetery to which people could arrive by intuition, nearly miraculously, and never by way of prescription. If people started to arrive by prescription, the place would start to get corrupted, and it would never recover.

The words rang in Lucas' fascinated ears. However, at the same time, deep inside him, bothering him as if being poked with a sharp stick, a worry plagued his conscience: what kind of report would he give to his superior about all of this?

Among other things, Ketelsen also spoke to them about the nonexistence of death. We typically believe in the existence of one room--the room of life. There is another room--the Great Beyond, Nothingness, God, or however you want to call it. Death is the door through which we go from one room to the next. What would happen if we were to prove that no such door existed? It would be absurd to dramatize it if it didn't exist. Tragedies exist only if they are recognized as such. Haven't all of us had the experience of being willing to give our lives for something or someone? Death was not intimidating to us at that point. Can we imagine how happy we would be if we were able to live that way permanently? We refer to our bodies as the real us. But before long that illusion, that mirage crumbles. Is your wife, your child, or a loved one in danger? You run to save him or her and you forfeit what is left of your body, and someone comes and picks it up like discarded, useless clothing. You offer yourself in place of the person you love and you don't have the sensation of having lost anything in the exchange. On the contrary, in the supposed sacrifice--which it never really is--you finally really find yourself. The danger which threatens your wife, child, or friend has destroyed not only the flesh, but worship of the flesh. That is the meaning of death which we need to regain, in this secret place, because--and he raised his long, bony index finger--the most important thing is to prove, recognize, *see* with our own eyes that we never die alone. Aloneness is merely an illusion. We are always surrounded by living beings for whom we live and die, but also by dead beings for whom we live and die, beings that could manifest themselves at any moment, but particularly at the moment we die.

⁜ ⁜ ⁜

"THAT CHILD…, THAT child…" Alberto was speaking as he sat on his chair, humpbacked, doubled over, and with a few white hairs bristling around the pinkish skin of his head and the mask of wrinkles on his face. He wore a well-tailored vest and suit coat. Why did he bother wearing them in the middle of the mountains, Lucas asked himself. "I am going to die, but I am not dead yet and I have come here to get help with it. I no longer have anything to do here. For centuries I have been living in the winter of old age, as I like to call it, when no thing and nobody can sweeten up my life. Even my memories start to disappear. 'Don't you realize that you are porous?' I tell myself each time I forget something. 'Don't you realize that an old damaged pitcher can't retain anything any more…?' Do you know when I stopped going to the club I had been going to for years? It was when I said hello twice to the same friend and he looked at me in such a mocking way that I couldn't stand it. Starting at that moment I discovered that if my hand shook when I put a coffee cup down on a table, that tremor was mockingly noticed by everyone around me. Or when I knelt down during mass, people noticed that I struggled to get up. It was awful. My legs, which can still walk down the street very well, can no longer perform the lovely task of bringing me upright in a leap. Nothing hurts me as much as being told I look good, despite my age. 'You're looking exceptionally good,' they say as they look at me sideways. SOBs! People who say that know perfectly well that nobody believes them, and all I can do is give a forced smile, practically a disgusted grin. People praise the appearance of an old man while no one would think of trying to convince a hunchback that his back is flat. What a relief it was to get back to my own room at night, where people could no longer judge me. I suspect it's the same for other people in my situation. At some point we become ageless because we go back to being what we have always been. We know the real self enough to know that we are not really any different, in the sunset of our lives, from the young men we used to be with locks of black hair on our foreheads. That hair used to be a marvelous passport certifying youthfulness--in any place and in any situation. No one asks for identification any more--it isn't necessary. People know just by looking at us that we are aliens from another world... Ah, but when we are alone and no one sees us but ourselves, we know who we are and feel no need to convince anybody of anything. We know that we haven't turned into something else... Oh, the permanence of the soul! Oh, to identify with ourselves fully, from time immemorial and forever! A friend of mine, also advanced in years, used to tell me that our childhood walks slower than we do. Think about that: our childhood walks more slowly than we do, and it can only catch up to us in the final years of our lives. When it does finally catch us, the child we used to be falls into step with us and holds our hand, as if to cross one last street..." His voice broke, he doubled over even more in his chair, and his chin jutted forward. "That child... that child is what I came here to find."

WHEN THE SESSION ended, Lucas explained to Ketelsen the purpose of his visit, the detailed report he was to make to his superior on the odd geography of the place, a survey of the people there, the sessions, and of course their activities. Ketelsen looked at him with an air of conspiracy and invited him to take a walk with him.

In the moonlight Lucas saw that Ketelsen's face was riddled with worry. He lit a cigarette. Puffs of smoke spiraled upward, then slowly distended and became part of the fog. He said that when he arrived in San Sóstenes there was nothing more than empty or partially damaged houses, shanties leaning against train cars with rusty sheets of metal as roofs, untilled land, chopped down forests, burnt areas, plots of land in which no one planted a single seed, empty stockyards between four fences made of spiny mesquite and animal bones. The vicarage, for example, was a large home in ruins. The rain would enter through broken roof tiles, slide down the walls, staining them and saturating them with moisture creating a breeding ground for mildew. The glacial wind from the mountains would beat on the exhausted doors and enter through glassless windows.

That was how sad San Sóstenes was when Ketelsen arrived. Now, thanks to working together with the Indians, it had been transformed into a fertile, productive place, in which no one was lacking for a bit of dry meat, corn, rice, pinole, sugar, prickly pears, medicines, friends, or relief from their problems. They had even successfully started some peach orchards. He should drop by the vicarage to see how they had transformed it. Each and every home was likewise being rejuvenated there. Had he noticed the way that they sparkled from a distance? Whitewashing them had made the entire locale take on an entirely different look. Don't you think they look good, Father Caraveo?

Ketelsen added in a more confidential tone, with a voice that he unsuccessfully tried to muffle, that in that privileged place he felt differently than in any other. It had a vivid luminosity even at night, with bright and contrasting colors, an extreme climate and constant murmurs that came up from the earth, and above all else the imposing, otherworldly existence of the mountains. As he said this, his prominent nose, like that of a predatory eaglet, seemed to examine the surrounding smells.

"What we plant here is for our own consumption (as you have surely noted, in this place we are all the same, whether Indians or whites), and the timber that we sell is to buy what the community needs. No one does business with anything or anybody. Everything belongs to whoever needs it first."

Never had a sky seemed so close to Lucas, nor the clusters of stars so within the reach of his hand. They took a little path among the pine trees, where silence was only broken by tiny sounds--the crunching of dry leaves under their feet, the bleating of a suckling lamb, the clamor of a squirrel climbing a tree, the crackle of a falling acorn. Lucas felt a dizzyness bubble up in his brain as he listened to Ketelsen, who had to steady his arm. Lucas recognized the energy in Ketelsen's movements, the determination he had seen in his eyes, and thought that even with that minimal contact with his hand he could discern the toughness of his bones and the magnetism of his touch.

Was Lucas familiar with the message that Karl Gustaph Jung left in one of his final letters? He said that perhaps the only way we could save ourselves as a species would be to insert into ourselves a new organ that had *physical* properties that would remind us, constantly, that we could die in the next instant, that we could not be assured of living even one more moment. It was akin to what had been attempted with the Roman emperors to return them to raw reality: "You are mortal, you are mortal, you are mortal." But also, above all, to remind us that the same thing is at work and will always be at work in our fellow beings, or better put our near beings, all those living beings we encounter on our way, no matter our circumstances. Perhaps then, thanks to that new organ, men would stop being so ambitious and cruel, and it would awaken in them compassion and pity for everything and everyone. That was not so different from what they were trying to accomplish in the confession groups, wouldn't he agree? Only a recognition of that type, and above all the physical sensation that would accompany it, could perhaps counteract our infinite, destructive, self-destructive selfishness.

"So only a place such as this, a place of transcendence, of scientific and religious experimentation--such a place could only exist in these marvelous, extraordinary mountains," he said emphatically.

"Do you really believe that such a place could exist only in the Tarahumara mountains, Father?"

Ketelsen nodded his head in the affirmative. As an Indian had confessed to him once, "Tata God has made us the way we are. We have always been the way you see us. We don't need to be baptized because in this place there is no devil."

"This is a detail we cannot overlook. Evil has no place here. The devil is a figure completely outside the Tarahumara conception of the world because it is entirely free of guilt. The devil could only be understood if he were present among them. 'He who lives below' made the *chabochis*, while 'he who lives above' made them, the *rarámuris*. Do you understand, Father Caraveo, that Tarahumara Indian lands were perhaps the only ones on the planet where one could not find greed or spite. Where else could you have a child summon a man accused of a crime, and that man follows the child meekly for miles until he can appear before the *siríame* to clarify the situation. Where else do trials reach resolution with reconciliation between the accused and the aggrieved parties because no one objects to asking forgiveness when asking forgiveness is in order? How long had it been since that capacity had been lost 'down there?'" and he pointed, as he did so many other times, at the ground, perhaps at the very center of the earth. "For the Tarahumaras, free from the guilt of the original sin, forgiveness never lessens them as people or humiliates them. To the contrary. The expression *wikála tána* does not mean just asking forgiveness, but also giving thanks to the Lord for what He has given us, for the grace he bestows upon us. They are completely free from competition, from ownership, and from ambition for power. Perhaps that is why they are at risk of extinction. Well, let's help them to survive so that they can help to save us."

"Do you really believe that the Tarahumaras can help to save us as a species, Father Ketelsen?" and Lucas paused for a moment to try to see his eyes in the darkness.

"I have no doubt about it. And they know it. That is why they sing:

Tamujé ko rarámuri ju	We are the *Rarámuris*
Tamujé lina noká iwébana gawi	We sustain the world
Tamujé ta ju gawí tónara	We are the pillar of the world.

If they, as the pillar of the world, were to break--and we should be careful because it could happen if we were to abandon them--the firmament would fall, crushing us all. The sun, the moon and the stars would plummet. There could be heavy snowfalls or rains that would flood and bury men everywhere. That is what they say and they do not doubt it."

"And you... you believe it?" Lucas asked almost offensively.

"Absolutely I believe it," and Ketelsen raised his shrill little voice to a fever pitch which left no room for doubt, "because believe me, they are the most unpretentious and most simple people in the world. They are a lot like Job when they pray: '*Tasi ta omonabo chiré nina aniriwe. Ne iwérapo cho chiré ta risua oriwae ko,*' which means 'We don't need to become sad if the *chabochis* make us suffer. We need to be happy even if they make us suffer.' And we truly have made them suffer and exploited their innate goodness to the point of infamy. They may not understand our theology, but they understand perfectly the words of Jesus: 'If any man desire to be first, the same shall be last of all, and servant of all.'" Ketelsen drew deeply on his cigarette and the ash lit up the shadows.

"And what have you accomplished through hypnosis?"

Ketelsen smiled. "Tomorrow I'll show you, when you are ready. I've used it not only with them, but with all our infirm and visitors who arrive here. It is true, as a matter of fact, that it is easier to hypnotize the Tarahumaras because of their way of looking at life, easier to call upon their ghosts, and to develop their telepathic capacities. The Tarahumaras *know* that we can separate the soul from the body and make it rise from the earth to the sky to receive strength from above and thus maintain a balance here below. They insist that dreams are the daily life of the soul--it leaves when the body sleeps, which is why the true desires of individuals can be found in their dreams. They know it without having to read Freud and Jung. They know that through their dreams people can discover their own spiritual state. Most importantly, they believe that some dreams are like direct conversations with their kindred dead and even with God, and that is why they consider people who do not dream dangerous and given over fully to physical matter."

Lucas shuddered as he thought about his recent nightmares. Ketelsen seemed to guess his thoughts because he immediately clarified: "Be careful about over-analyzing the 'journeys' of the soul in its dreams. Those 'journeys' are the most dangerous thing for the soul. Those lacking sufficient interior strength can 'lose it.' When that happens, the Tarahumaras call the shaman and ask him to leave his own body to go look for the lost soul. Have you ever seen that ceremony? It is most revealing."

Lucas answered that he had not, and said that the Indians were very careful to do certain religious ceremonies away from the Jesuit priests of the mission because they were afraid of being reprimanded, repressed, and punished.

Ketelsen took his arm, transmitting to Lucas an intense current of heat. "You don't realize what you have lost because of the prejudices of the Jesuits. What a shame. The current day Church is a danger to the salvation of souls. It is so preoccupied with maintaining and extending its power in this world that it is terrified of having contact with the 'other' world. It is a Church that Christ has abandoned, so we need to look for Him wherever we can." And with a sweeping gesture he pointed out the mountains and the night. "Rilke says that Christ returned to men as an 'anti-death' being. You can verify that here, Father."

Together they gazed heavenward and Lucas discovered that the tip of a pine tree was oscillating between Sirius and the Little Dipper, and seemed to be chasing the latter away. Curiously, at that exact moment Ketelsen started talking about the stars. "When we observe a constellation we are more or less aware of the harmony, the rhythm that unites its stars and makes it more than the simple sum of those stars. Haven't you noticed that lone stars, the ones that don't form a part of a constellation, seem less brilliant and sadder? Humankind must have sensed from the beginning of time that each constellation was like a clan, or an ethnicity. You should see how the Tarahumaras are amazed as they look at the stars. You can see it in the eyes of children also, but we lose it as we grow older. The same thing happens with the movements of clouds." Ketelsen said for that very reason he enjoyed going to the train station--the one right on the outskirts of town--to watch people arrive. "One can spend hours standing on the landing, observing people coming and going, trying to discern the possible order within the terrible chaos which surrounds us. Trying to sense things before they happen influences them, gives them a path. It constitutes another type of encounter; it is the mystery that makes us what we are. Incalculably separate destinies suddenly unite, arriving from remote and dissimilar places, bringing together the loneliness of individuals and converting them into –here and now, which is our permanent motto—one united body, into a constellation."

"That you and I are here together is a good example, Father Caraveo. Can our encounter be entirely coincidental?" The cigarette butt Ketelsen flicked into the air did pirouettes in the darkness, mimicking a firefly.

"I was actually baptized with the name Ambrosio, but since I knew so much about Benito Juárez in the Guachochi School, they started

41

to call me Benito and the name Benito has stuck." He was an elderly Indian, barefoot and with tousled hair under a soiled headscarf. "I'm going to die because I am very sad since I lost my daughter. She got lost on the other side of the hill, over by the little waterfall. She got lost because it was raining a lot. She told me so in dreams. When it stopped raining the mountains became engulfed in fog. She couldn't see, it became late, and she went into a cave to go to sleep, inside the mountain. And she couldn't come out because her dream wouldn't let her. The goats made their way back to the house alone. In the family we didn't realize it. We thought she had just gone to stay at a different house, which is what happens quite a bit in these parts with children, and that's why we don't go looking for them. I've wondered why I didn't immediately go out and look for her, but that gets me nowhere. From the time that she was a little girl my daughter had dreams about people who had died. She would talk with them. In the San Sóstenes School she had nurtured her abilities to cast out *rusíwaris*, evil spirits, from homes and other places. But she went to sleep in the mountains and she died. Later we found her remains. Since then, in dreams, I've spoken with her and I've told her that I want to see her again, that I am dying from the sadness of not seeing her. A curandero tried to heal me, but couldn't. He put his heavy, warm breath all over my body, in a long ceremony. He cracked my knuckles, my wrists, and my ankles, but didn't accomplish a thing. In my dreams my daughter has told me not to die, to wait for a while, but I tell her that sadness is going to kill me if I don't see her and there is nothing I can do about it. So in the last dream, we agreed that I would go to where she is. What I don't know is how I am going to die, although sadness kills in a hurry. There is no need for an illness to come to our aid when we want to die. Sometimes a person decides something during a dream and it is impossible to change his mind when he is awake.

✠ ✠ ✠

KETELSEN AND LUCAS went to the church. They crossed a large square with old pine trees which, buffeted by gusts of night time wind, creaked like the timbers on a ship. The cloister adjacent to the chapel served as Ketelsen's vicarage and bedroom. On the columns some heavy ocote candles were burning, giving off large flames, spitting out sparks, and smelling of resin. The room was large, humid, and very clean. The imposing architecture of three loaded bookshelves rose above the rest of the simple furniture. There was a narrow cot with a wooden cross above it. Opposite the window with its blankets for curtains there was a table-desk with a lectern for books, an old friar's chair, and a kerosene lamp. A thick but frayed and faded cotton rug swallowed up the sound of footsteps and suggested a sweet invitation to solitude. Lucas went over to the books and Ketelsen confessed his vice of collecting them, mentioning that what they were seeing there was but a small part of his collection. Those books contained all the possible illuminations of the soul, all the madnesses of intellect, all the logical reasonings and the most blasphemous audaciousness to which men had arrived in their search for meaning for this and the next life. That is where Ketelsen looked for the Absolute, although he did not know for sure whether he was seeking refuge in love or in fear, in faith or in the doubts of his faith. He read those books with a voracity that became more intense as he would find in them a reflection of his own feelings or answers to his burnings questions. He followed a strict regimen of vigil and sleep which obeyed only the law imposed by his readings. He experienced unexpected illuminations or collapses due to his studies, which danced around him like little demons. The path of his moral perdition was certainly well marked, in the opinion of his ecclesiastical superiors. He encouraged Lucas to look at that section in particular, as it had so much to do with his current work there in the mountains, despite it being a hodgepodge collection: <u>The Ark had a Vineyard as a Candle</u> by Lanza del Vasto, <u>Island</u> by Aldeous Huxley, <u>Christianopolis: An Ideal State of the Seventeenth Century</u> by Johann Andreae, <u>Erewhon</u> by Samuel Butler, <u>The Theory of the Four Movements</u> by Charles Fourier, <u>The City of the Sun</u> by Tomasso Campanella, <u>If this is Utopia</u> by Henry Neville, <u>The Notebooks of Malte Laurids Brigge</u> by Rilke, <u>The World Will be a Paradise</u> by Lit Zun, <u>Death</u> by Elisabeth Kubler-Ross, <u>The New Atlantis</u> by Francis Bacon, <u>Other Worlds: The Comical History of the States and Empires of the Moon and Sun</u> by Cirano de Bergerac, <u>The Buried Temple</u> by Maeterlinck, <u>The Seven Storey Mountain</u> by Thomas Merton...

Ketelsen took out a small leather-covered book and went directly to a passage marked by the page's folded corner.

"Listen to what Antonin Artaud says about our mountains: 'I have seen here, in Norogachi, deep in the Tarahumara Mountains, the realization of the ritual of the kings of Atlantis, that race of mysterious and magical origins. I have no doubt that the Tarahumaras are direct descendants of Atlantis and they are still dedicated to the cult of those magical rites, with complete devotion. Only they could do so. I have seen in the Tarahumara mountains *the entire ritual* of those fanciful and desperate kings.' What do you think of that, Father? Listen to Artaud's conclusion: 'If it is true what the Tarahumaras themselves claim, that they have fallen directly *from heaven to the earth*, it can be said that they have fallen into a nature that was prepared for them ahead of time.'"

Ketelsen emphasized that: a nature that was prepared for them ahead of time. To truly understand one has to wonder about that Atlantis of which Artaud spoke. Wasn't it simply a symbol of lost unity, of time before time, the non-time prior to history and the original sin, the "other" time, the time of confrontation and resurrection in agony through the King of Death, as Artaud also mentioned? Lucas was trying to remember as best he could Ketelsen's words for the report he would make to his superior. At the moment he could sense that the reference to the King of Death was stretching the corners of his mouth into a sarcastic grimace.

Had Lucas read <u>Bardo Todol</u>? "No? Listen to this, Father. At the moment someone who has recently died is judged, the King of Death presents him with a simple mirror… But it is a mirror which actually reveals his karma, or the totality of his actions. In that mirror he sees reflected, as if watching a movie within himself, all his actions, whether good or bad. The key is that the reflection does not correspond to any exterior reality, but rather it is a projection of mental images, of that which in the occult is called the subtle body. What a term, don't you think?"

"Very clever, yes" Lucas acknowledged with a forced smile.

"The King of Death looks into the mirror, but what he is really seeing is the memory of the deceased."

"Wouldn't it be easier to just confess?" Lucas ventured to ask.

"The problem is that in the Catholic religion God is an exterior, omniscient being who issues a final judgment, either of salvation or condemnation. By contrast, in the <u>Bardo Todol</u>, the judgment pronounced by the King of Death does not originate with him, but with the deceased himself, from his mental body."

"Do you really still believe, Father? I mean, you still officiate at mass, you hypnotize and baptize Indians, you impart the sacraments, but do you really still believe in God? I'm asking you this because it is precisely the central dilemma of my life." Lucas half-closed his eyes with that look which can only be learned in suspenseful movies.

A tiny wrinkle appeared between Ketelsen's eyebrows and he showed Lucas the palms of his hands.

"What does it mean to believe any more, Father Caraveo? It is said that it is impossible for human beings to tolerate an imperfect God, who is being created and is evolving with us. I would say that faith, at least the way I live it, is not an insurance firm for weak, needy people. My faith is based on an elevated, courageous spirit. Only in that way can we understand that, in the course of our evolution, and with the growing understanding of ourselves and each other, we start to become aware that we are part of the struggle for Divinity and coauthors thereof. Always coauthors."

"Pure Teilhard de Chardin."

"He was also a Jesuit priest, by the way. Although I prefer a faith which is less philosophical and more concrete, like the faith of the character created by Graham Greene who was asked to describe his faith in God, and he modestly responded: 'I do not believe in God. I have contact with him.'"

Lucas changed the subject by looking over a gallery of yellowed photographs that covered much of the opposite wall and asked if they were relatives.

"Most of them are. I'll be reunited with them on the 'other side.'" Ketelsen clarified: "I hope to be with some very good friends on the other side also."

It was a virtual family ossuary, complete with chapters of passion and tears, reduced now to faded heads with hair that was slicked back or decorated with curls, grand gestures, profiles that had managed to hold their ardor or languor for the long seconds of a pose. An invisible eye had captured for the benefit of posterity emphatic or timid looks. It had framed all shades of love or family discontent. An instant perpetuated in sepia on the wall, evoking for the survivor, perhaps in the most vivid way possible, the re-encounter imminent in the other world (or would it happen in this world?).

Ketelsen went to his table-desk, lit a cigarette, his other impregnable vice, he said, and invited Lucas to sit down also for a bit. "Tell me about yourself, Father Caraveo, about how you became a priest."

Lucas finally felt a little more at ease, thanks to the tranquility of the furniture and books, to Ketelsen's tone of voice, and he felt the calm became even softer in the carpet under his feet.

"I became a priest as a vocation, I believe. Although my mother undoubtedly influenced me. I know Freud would have something to say about that. She was a lady and member of all the religious societies in Chihuahua. As a child raised smelling incense, constantly seeing the robes of the devout and the bustle of the sacristy, I readily considered the path of the priesthood. It makes sense, doesn't it? In addition to flights of sentimentality, the enthusiastic effusion so common in adolescents can be interpreted as a call to Grace. For some, that kind of emotion finds its way naturally into a brothel, into alcohol, or a sudden love affair. But in a young man completely lacking money, timid, virtually friendless, tied to his mother's apron strings, there was no other path but that of a novitiate."

Lucas also told him about his long journey in the mountains, how he fainted, and the feeling of anguish which he couldn't shake. He emphasized his theological doubts, the failure of his priestly vocation, the awful sensation he had that an immense fissure was about to open at his feet, an abyss that would envelope him. What he lived the day before in the mountains was but a symbol for the whole, he believed. And in his fall he would be unable to claim either the merit of a sacrifice freely given and carried out, or the fecundity of martyrdom. It was going to be like the fall of a rock into a well. A dark echo and nothing else. Could it be that he had not been able to become reconciled to his shadow, as Saint Ignatius of Loyola would put it?

Using his tongue, Ketelsen pushed his cigarette to the side of his mouth, which broke out into a sudden, kind smile.

"My goodness, Father Caraveo, I now understand why you came here. For the time being, become deserving of that anguish which eats at you day and night. Don't fight it. Trust me. Tell yourself that you are in anguish and that it's good. Become worthy of it. If you can locate it and recognize it, tracking it from moment to moment, if you can even manage to love it and thank the Lord for it, then you can be free from its most damaging effects, and it will prod you toward transcendence, to *see* what you have to *see*."

"Become worthy of it?" asked Lucas, feeling that just by bringing up the subject his mouth started to dry out and that drops of sweat appeared on his forehead.

Ketelsen crushed his cigarette butt in the ashtray and Lucas started to say goodbye, since it was his first night there and it seemed wisest to him. He knew how to get home, Susila had explained it to him in detail, on the other side of the church, everyone had been very kind, he could use a little more of a walk. Ketelsen invited him to the next day's activities, which would include an attempt to communicate with someone on *the other side* through a seriously ill individual in a mountain cave.

"My God, you want me to witness an attempt to communicate with someone on *the other side* through a seriously ill individual in a mountain cave, in the anguished state I am in? Imagine it, Father Ketelsen."

"It might be advantageous. Either you will get better or you will become thoroughly terrified. But you'll get better, you'll see."

Lucas made a face that tried to turn into a smile, with the corners of his nose slowly wrinkling up.

"What a dilemma. What do they call your system? Shock therapy?"

LUCAS WALKED AROUND the town for a few minutes before going to bed. He thought about how peaceful and clean everything was up there, about the deep sky, studded with stars, and about the contrast with the tumult and permanent agony, more than anything else, down below. On the way he found a group of people curled up around a fire, the reddish tongues of which danced with the wind. Their faces were extremely varied in their shapes and colors. They called to him and Lucas joined them, greeting them with a tilt of his head and a timid smile. He suddenly found himself in the center of a circle of inquisitive but kind faces. Smiles and hands to shake spontaneously reached out to him. There was excitement as everyone wanted to talk with the newcomer. They asked him about his trip and the illness he undoubtedly had. What illness was it? A Tarahumara Indian, without saying a word, put into his hands a steaming bowl of fried goat meat, sprinkled with corn flour; a man with thick, perhaps tinted eyebrows, handed him a container of tesgüino. They all drank the liquid in an attitude of participating in a ritual, and Lucas followed suit.

"How long do you have to live?" someone wrapped up in a blanket asked him, with a naturalness that was disarming. The man's face was full of stretch marks, his skin looked like wax, and his entire body seemed fragile.

The food seemed to get stuck in Lucas' mouth and he answered more with a forced smile than with words: "How can I know? Sometimes it's hard to know."

"What have doctors told you?" asked an old man, flashing without shame his wilted gums. "What did they tell you 'down there?'"

"Sometimes they say one thing and then they say another. You know how that goes. You know better than anyone."

"Once Ketelsen looks you over, he'll tell you how much time you have left to live, you'll see," said a plump man who covered his mouth with three fingers, covering a cavernous cough.

"The doctors had given up on me--they gave me just three months to live," said a woman. Beneath a layer of excessive makeup he could make out another face, a sadder and sweeter one, which was looking at him as if from under water. "Ketelsen told me that he is not a witch doctor and he doesn't perform miracles, but he hypnotized me, removed the cause of my sadness, and now I have been here for over a year feeling very well. Just look at me."

A man then spoke whose face was twisted and had eyes which were unusually far apart, almost as if they belonged to two different faces. "I placed myself into the care of some folk healers, who looked into my blood flow, they gathered facts, they invoked who knows what, but accomplished nothing. I breathed in the aromatic smoke of herbs that were supposedly miraculous, but nothing. Until Ketelsen asked me: 'Where did your path take a turn? Where did you get off course? Where did your spirit become afraid?' And I told him everything."

"Even if Ketelsen tells you he is not a witch doctor and doesn't perform miracles, insist on having him hypnotize you. You'll see that he can even take you back to a prior life," counseled the plump man with the cavernous cough, with slow, extremely slow words, which were separated by the complaining air of his breathing.

Lucas tried to smile, in light of his situation, not suffering any illness, inventing ills that he had never experienced, speaking about physicians and specialists about whom he had no idea, but he did so only from his teeth outward. That was because fear, that evil thing, as Saint Ignatius of Loyola called it, continued inside him. There was no need to try to fool himself. It even seemed to grow larger and branch out, like one of the tumors the inhabitants of that place discussed so much. His hands trembled, he shivered and inched steadily closer to the fire to heat up the ice he felt inside. He thought "You are going to die of fright, Lucas." The huge drops of sweat, the shivers, the iciness, and the shakes he was experiencing were all part of a panic a person feels, or senses, when death is near. But it was an absurd fear because he wasn't even sick--at least he was not aware of it if he was--and the grave dangers he had experienced in the mountains were now in his past. Or was he actually sick, like everyone else there, and that is why he managed to find the place? Indeed, he had lost so much weight in just a few hours that his pants were baggy and his shirt was sliding all over. Or was it just this place? The faces, the excessive makeup, the words of the confession group, the hazy aura that surrounded everyone there.

He accepted a little more tesgüino, and while she served it to him, the Indian woman offered him some advice: "If you already feel a little high, have some esquite. That will dampen the way you feel and you can drink more."

The wind continued its unflagging battle with the rebel flames. One of the Indians dug into his clothing and pulled out an awkwardly made flute of ash. A single musical note, tense and continuous, slowly took on meaning, transformed into a second note, then yielded to a melody which returned and became lost in a chord which was increasingly richer and happier, as if it were accompanied by invisible instruments. A young Indian woman, who looked very healthy, accompanied the music by clapping, doing little hops, nearly doing a little dance. Her look, her hands, her dark skin seemed effervescent. Another woman, wearing a dress that was absurd for the time and place, full of ruffles, followed her, imitating the song in Tarahumara. As she sang, she would finish each chorus with a kind of cry. Eventually everyone was singing and dancing. The mountains, towering over them, seemed to send magnificent, resounding echoes back to them. When Lucas departed their group, no one even noticed.

THE TESGÜINO HAD made him feel better, considerably better, and he walked randomly in the night, with the town silent, free even from the sound of dogs barking or the mooing of restless cattle. He felt a quiet chill, as if the wind had fallen asleep in the buttresses of the mountains. Why the sudden silence? On only one other occasion had he drunk tesgüino, when he had recently arrived as a novitiate, and it had the same effect. People, houses and trees were real images, they belonged to the real world, but at the same time they floated, deformed, in a misty, burning atmosphere; they took on an entirely new aspect, a fourth dimension of sorts. He walked until the final houses of the town, where the flatness started to rise up, to undulate, covered by terribly dry grass.

He found the station at the exact moment a train was arriving, emanating like a tremor from the mountains. It bedazzled him and he instinctively felt like raising his hand to order the train to stop.

The train did exist. The iron tracks, lacking ballast, writhed like snakes. When the train went past it stirred up dust, which got into his eyes and further clouded his vision.

The train's bright light, like a shooting star, the steam that came from the pistons, and the deafening squeal of iron on iron parted the night into two. The sound of a shrill whistle came from the distance.

Lucas rubbed his eyes and approached one of the initial cars.

He could see silhouettes through its large windows, but a violet light lent them a vague shade of purplish, gelatinous quicksilver, like a crude plaster mask.

Each silhouette seemed to be installed in a bubble, as if slowly moving in an aquarium, all lined up and translucent.

Voices and peals of laughter could be heard in the upper parts of the train, which traveled upward into the motionless layers of air.

Lucas trembled and stepped backward, and at that moment the large dark torso of a man approached the window. His large and immobile profile was readily recognizable, enough to clearly distinguish his features and the expression of his eyes.

Lucas turned his head before the man could look into his eyes and started hurriedly back to the town.

That was enough for one night, he thought. Why belabor what he already knew? Nothing could change his premonitions. He needed to quiet his sense of anguish and anxiety. He needed to sleep a bit and put into practice the stoic resignation that Ketelsen preached.

THE TINY, NEBULOUS circles of his extinguished, inexpressive pupils contrasted with his healthy, communicative face, with the lively movement of his hands, and with his intense voice. He paused on occasion, creating silences which enhanced his story and gave it substance which then floated down to his listeners like falling ash.

"When I lost my sight I set out to get rid of space and time with a type of indifferent immobility. Have you noticed that we feel the passage of time less when we are tranquil and relaxed? I nearly achieved my desire, but it came at a high price, because I became excessively aware of the complex mechanism of life inside each of us, causing our blood to circulate, our livers to secrete bile, our pancreas to regulate our sugar, our kidneys to produce urine, and our muscles to move at our whim. Even my dreams became too vivid and I would often see myself sleeping, then I would enter into my dream world. In one such dream I found out that I was going to die. I saw myself dead. And that is why I immediately came here. It was a dream in which I was regaining my sight (I dream that a lot) and I marveled as I looked at the full moon over the mountains. I followed a vague path to a river, and then slowly walked along its banks with the sensation of being shoeless and my feet would sink into the mud. In that dream I was alone in the mountains, which is strange because I always dream that I am with someone. If I were to have that dream again, I am certain that the solitude I felt would not feel so negative any more. That dream was one thing *there* and it would be something entirely different *here*. You are all aware of the special solitude here in the mountains, of the moon which grows larger by the instant as it rises above the hills, of the splashing of the river and the sound of frogs. I walked to a place where my feet found more solid soil. I stopped to take a nice long look at the water. The entire river was a moon, an enormous and confusing set of knives that slashed at my eyes as if to blind me again, but this time in my dream. It was trying to stop me from seeing what I was destined to see--my body floating in the river, breaking free from some branches and entering into the current, then drifting to the edge of the river visible in the full moon. I then felt overwhelmed by anguish unlike any I had ever felt and I realized there was no point in staying where I was. Then I came to be here with all of you."

LUCAS AWOKE TO knocking on the door when dawn was nothing more than a touch of blue on the horizon. When he opened his eyes, the world put itself together before his eyes with the precision of a complex puzzle. He jumped out of bed and went to open the door. In jumbled Spanish and hand signals, a Tarahumara child told him that Susila was waiting for him in the sanitarium, and to hurry because someone had just died and he was invited to the ceremony they were organizing. The boy said he would show him the way but he had to come immediately. The morning light reflected in the boy's dark eyes, which were shaking as if in a windstorm. He wore jeans with large patches at the knees.

Susila had left him some water in a washbasin and he managed to wash up a bit. He got dressed and left as quickly as possible. He heard the chirping of birds, the day's first buzz of bugs and many other confused, varied, increasing sounds. The sun was starting to beat upon the whitewashed homes. As he passed by them he thought he could imagine their rhythmic hearts: darkness in which pleasant women laughed and gave the first orders of the day, sunny patios brightened by children and their games, and pens with animals shaking off the night. It was as if all were inaugurating the world afresh. Golden leaves fell off oak trees then glided through the air, little pieces of death, he thought.

"Here comes the teacher," said the boy, then he vanished.

The scene of death which he found in one of the little hospital rooms, despite its silence, seemed to him a continuation of the phantasmagoric yet chatty series of images thrust upon him the night before, in the confession group. On a cement slab there was an unclothed male cadaver--middle-aged, olive skin, arms hanging to the sides as if exhausted. The eyes were wide open and fixed on a point on the ceiling. Nothing else was in the room. Just white walls, a small window and two other empty cement slabs. As Lucas entered, he felt that he was violating an intimacy, that he had no right to be there, for Heaven's sake, with a recently deceased man who didn't even have a sheet over him. Why do naked cadavers seem even more naked than they ever could have been in life? He looked for something to cover the man, but found nothing.

He became nervous, started to twirl his thumbs, and made an effort to look elsewhere in the room. But his eyes were always drawn back to the dead man. It seemed like part of a macabre joke –could it be just that?—that they would lead him there alone, there of all places, standing before the embodiment of his worst fears. Of course he could leave the room and wait for Susila outside, but did he want to? He took a pair of steps toward the cement slab. He studied the stretched-out man: his lines were already becoming sharper, like the edges of a rock. His skin was starting to take on an opaque, clay-like hue. A chill and silence seemed to be rising out of that recently abandoned machine. But what impressed him most profoundly were the man's eyes: bulging, perhaps about to burst because of what they last saw, growing darker by the instant and almost becoming covered with rust. The mouth seemed to be trying to emit one last impossible complaint which was caught forever within. In what he considered a tiny act of modesty, he closed the man's eyes.

He remembered his father, dead now for years. The setting was very different because they held his wake in a funeral home in the city of Chihuahua. How could he not remember that long overnight vigil with a loved one who both was and wasn't in this world, in darkness scarcely affected by a little lamp with a purple shade that blocked the light rather than encouraging it. He could practically bring back the thick smell of funeral flowers and melting wax. The early morning awakened from its vast silence, broken by the muffled yawn of someone who had fallen asleep. Lucas remembered. He remembered.

His mother lost her composure when she looked in the coffin for the last time. "The poor thing," she bawled, "Look at how he has left us! Look at how he has left us! He suffered to the very end! What evil did he do for God to make him suffer so much? The poor thing!"

When he saw his mother in that state, he went to console her and also to look in the coffin. His eyes did not want to, neither could they contemplate for long that face he loved so dearly, now extinguished forever, so pointy and pale that it seemed a caricature of his father. A swirl of pleasant and painful memories started to churn in Lucas' memory, staggering around and bumping into each other in his mind. When his conscience started to stumble because of unbearable anguish, he felt that a mixture of a shriek and a scream was making its way from his heart to his throat. But he silenced it, biting his lips, as he knew that if he shouted it would simply complicate things for his mother. He simply hugged her tight, and moved her little by little away from the coffin, from the mountain of unbearable memories.

He was jolted out of his thoughts by the sudden and noisy arrival of a group of children--later on he learned that they were Susila's students--mostly Tarahumara Indians. If a horse had entered at gallop, Lucas thought, it could not have invaded that space with such a feeling of desecration. Why was a loud and laughing group of children here?

"Settle down, quiet down, stop pushing," Susila ordered. "Get into a line and go past him one by one. One at a time, please."

Susila went over to the cement slab and with a vehemence that Lucas would not have imagined, exclaimed, "Who closed the eyes of the cadaver?"

"I did," replied Lucas, embarrassed.

"You did a bad thing. A very bad thing. You ruined our class."

"Please forgive me. It seemed like a tiny act of modesty on his behalf."

"What does modesty have to do with closing the eyes of a man who just died? Now the children won't be able to say goodbye to him as they would have liked."

Lucas didn't answer. What would have been the point? He simply kept standing by the door, wrapped up in himself. Susila repeated the instructions to her students.

"No pushing. One at a time."

The children complied and, although they still had some giggles and made some gestures to each other, they largely quieted down. First they recited a prayer together, which sounded much better than Lucas had expected. Susila, at the head of the cadaver, then repeated the Lord's prayer for what seemed to be a very long time.

The children walked past the naked cadaver, touched the face and kissed it! He heard one of the children say, "We love you. Goodbye, friend, we'll see you soon."

Susila also spoke to the cadaver: "Now you can let go. Let go of everything. Shake free of that old body that you no longer need. Let it be. Go toward the light, go, go."

The children stroked the face, the head, the hair, and the chest and arms. They kissed the forehead and cheeks. Each one whispered a farewell then gave the sign of the cross before vacating the spot for the next classmate. And then they went back to their giggling and childhood antics.

Before they left, Susila explained to Lucas that children need to be taught to become familiar with death, to see it up close, to get used to it, to confront it face to face, to speak to it, to remove from it, as much as possible, its tragic feeling, that tragic feeling that, in her opinion, was simply a lack of faith in *something beyond*.

"And can you prove to the children that there is *something beyond?*"

"Of course we can," Susila answered indignantly. "You'll see it in due time."

"From the time I was a child I had that gift: when I heard a stream, I knew whether or not it was happy. I could tell that a plant didn't like people to look at it. Those clouds are melancholy. Sometimes I could look into the eyes of certain people and I knew all about the state of their health. I could talk to owls if I smoked peyote or drank enough tesgüino. When I grew older, this gift was magnified and they made me a *sipame*. I healed many people, but one day I discovered a child sitting next to the river, bundled up in a blanket, watching over his flock of goats, playing with rocks and acorns, in his own little world. From a long ways off I saw that he was strange. When he threw a rock into the water, I saw that his soul had left his body, that one of those beings that live in the bottom of rivers had taken his soul along with the rock. It hadn't taken his entire soul, but most of it was gone, and what was left was not enough for him to be healthy. That's why he was sick. I went over to see him, and to be able to look for his soul I had to remove my own soul from my body, which is always difficult and dangerous. I put my rosary into my tesgüino cup and then ran it over his body, blowing my breath at his heart. I breathed and breathed on his heart, but was unable to accomplish anything. With the help of the cross on my rosary, dripping the magical power of tesgüino, I popped his knuckles, his wrists, his knees and his ankles. I put my fingers, dripping with tesgüino, into his mouth. I started to drink it myself because I was feeling so weak. After I drank quite a bit, I felt very clearly that my soul was leaving my body, that it was going out into the night and into the river. My soul wandered through the depths of the river until it found the soul of the boy. But we couldn't find our way back to our bodies and a few days later the boy died. I have kept on drinking tesgüino all the time, every day, but I know that my soul isn't going to find its way back to my body, and that I should become resigned to the fact that my body is going to die without its soul."

THEY HEADED BACK toward the school which was several blocks away. Susila told the children to go eat breakfast, and they immediately and tumultuously disappeared. Susila and Lucas went into one of the first rooms at the school, in which there was a group of about 20 adolescents, predominantly Tarahumara also, who were in concentrated silence, their brows knit over their books and moving pencils. A large set of windows opened onto an interior courtyard, through which the sun poured in like a voracious fire which made the entire room burn. The students' desks were lined up facing the windows. In one corner, on a wooden crate, was a small model of the universe made out of cardboard and wire. Thanks to an ingenious mechanical system the nine planets revolved around a rubber sun. Susila's desk faced those of the students, and on it were a pile of books and notebooks. A large blackboard seemed even blacker near the door. After he was introduced to the class, Lucas sat in one of the vacant desks toward the back of the room. Susila opened a cardboard box to the side of her desk and asked the students to come and get their peach. After they had done so, holding a peach in her own hand she started to talk about the sense of touch. She told the students to lightly feel its texture, its silky skin. She said such astonishing things about the sense of touch that it seemed to Lucas that no other sense aspired with such ferocity to take direct possession of things: to touch them, grasp them, seize them, sometimes even take them apart, crush them, mash them, and put them into one's body. It is the most blind, most awkward and most disillusioned of the senses, but the least guilty. If we don't take things apart, if we resist the temptation to take them apart, everything we touch is good, or becomes good. What was that fruit made up of? The youthful hands were holding their pieces of fruit as if offering it at an altar. Now Susila directed them to create a new depiction of it, via a very different route, using a colored drawing. It wasn't to be a likeness like the one they had made before, and it was not to be like the one that was in their textbook. It should not even represent how a farmer would see a peach. No. They needed to break free from all of that. Would that be possible? They were to look at it with the greatest measure of innocence possible. They were to look at this infinitely miraculous item they had before them. Susila lifted her own peach up into a stream of light. Why did it exist? Why did it have to exist? Look at it as if you had never seen anything like it ever before. Above all else, pretend that it has no name. Look at it with all your faculties, wide awake, with your eyes open, but with a sense of calm receptivity, without comparing it or classifying it. Would that be possible? And as you look at it, inhale its mystery. The children responded, moving the fruit to their noses. That's right. Let that aroma inspire you to discover its mystery. Good. Now write what you have felt. They calmly obeyed. One of the children desperately bit his pencil. Now look at the peach again, and after looking at it, close your eyes. Squeeze your eyes shut with the image of the peach inside. Now draw it. Draw the fruit that you have in front of you, and also draw the fruit that you saw when your eyes were closed. Make two drawings. Are they the same? Draw it, poorly or well it doesn't matter, then color it. Use all the colors you want. You can make peaches any color you want. You can distort them, make them small, cut them up, take out their pits, give them eyes, hair, branches, leaves or whatever you want. Understood? Now let's try to do the most difficult thing of all, but the most important one for our game: look very intently into the eyes of the classmate you have next to you. Attach your eyes to each other. Good. Now shut your eyes. Open them again. Now try to draw the fruit that your classmate drew. It can be a surprise. Who would think of creating a peach like that, you'll probably think. It's quite different from the one you made, isn't it? Try it again. Compare the two drawings--the one that you saw and the one that your classmate saw. Look at the colors--which are the most vivid, or the most pale? How many colors did you each use and which ones? The students burst into laughter, with each laugh louder than the prior, when they compared drawings. Some were amazingly similar, while others were completely different, they reported. Finally, as was expected--and hoped for--Susila gave the order for them to eat their peaches, which they did indeed do, with enthusiasm.

BUT PERHAPS THE moment which surprised Lucas the most in the valley of San Sóstenes came when he helped officiate at a noon mass with Father Ketelsen. When he asked about the homily, Ketelsen said that he would start with a prayer for students of mystery. Lucas opened his eyes so far they almost popped out of his head.

"Why pray for students of mystery?"

Ketelsen pulled his robe across his chest and answered by handing him a small book which he said contained the prayers for the week. Lucas glanced at it. This was like gold for his supervisor, he thought.

Wednesday. For Students of Mystery. Let us pray for those who study and practice the science of mystery. Thanks to them, tradition has passed on to us the knowledge from the ancients and primitive revelations. May we be worthy, Lord, to take part in that heritage, to contemplate thy vestiges found in things: in numbers, in proportions, in harmonies, in the relationships between elements, in the chasms between high and low, in the virtues of plants, in the prophecies found in stars and dreams, in the signs inscribed in hands and faces, in animals, plants, metals and minerals, and in the place that each being occupies in the realm of the Being.

Thursday. For Buddhists. Let us pray for the faithful devotees of He who is smaller than the germ of a grain of rice and, at the same time, larger than all of the worlds and suns combined. Make us, Lord, like them, in their pious respect for thy tiniest creatures, in their knowledge of self, in their mental concentration, in their ascetic and devout strength. Oh Thou who hast no limits, oh Thou who hast no face, oh Thou who hast no name, who art distinct from all that is, who art not this nor that, and who art not nothingness; Thou, who rejecteth all who say "I," who art the absence of thirst and pain and desire and fear and ignorance and worry and injustice; my God, before whom it is better to remain silent than to say "my God," blessed be thou for this, thy open lotus upon the essential waters of wisdom.

Friday. For Dismembered Christianity. On this day which we make holy by penitence and in consideration of death and the cross, let us pray, brothers and sisters, for dismembered Christianity, which is crucifying Christ anew with each new division it creates. Let us uproot from within us the prideful prejudices which separate us and rend His sacred body. Our grudges open afresh His wounds and poison them. Our doctrinal disputes crown Him with thorns, hang Him on a nail, and shorten His breath. May the profundity and richness of the Church of the Orient, may the strength and spaciousness of the Church of Rome, may the sincerity and freshness of the reformed Churches and inspired new churches come together in a common offering and a new song. May the sheep of this fold and those of other folds simply come together to form one flock of the Good Shepherd.

Saturday. For Israel. On this day held sacred by the Hebrews and for their ancestors from the beginning of the world, let us pray that the Lord will remember His promise made to Abraham and his seed throughout the ages. Let us pray for the children of Israel, that they may remember constantly their eternal God, the word of God, the law of God, the just and terrible demands of a jealous God upon His promised people. We are indebted to the Hebrews for that which is most precious to us: God Himself, the true God, the only God, the living God, He whose name is what-it-is. Have so many of them died, been sacrificed, so that perhaps through their blood we may have the right to their inheritance? And those still living are our benefactors because they have given us the Bible, and our Savior was one of them. May it please the Almighty to find us all once again united upon the holy ground of mount Zion and in eternal tabernacles.

Sunday. For the Catholic Church. Let us pray for our holy mother, the Catholic, Apostolic, Roman church. Let us pray to God that He will defend her from her enemies, the worst of which is our lukewarm natures. May He unite it, purify it, and give it life. Let us remember the promise that was given to us through her: that the gates of Hell shall never prevail. Let us remember the promised gift: the keys to open the Heavens and the Earth; to open hearts and make bare souls. Let us remember the bridge: the seven pillars of the bridge of the sacraments. Let us remember the ransom: the bread and the wine as the flesh and spirit. Let us remember the testimony: of the Saints that make it flourish in every season, and our time cannot be the exception. Let us remember revelation: the science which all science overlooks, which deals with the beginning and end of everything, the resurrection. I have loved, Lord, the beauty of Thy house and the mansion of Thy glory. May the walls be composed of transparent topaz and amethyst and may it be illuminated from within and not shed any darkness.

Monday. For Muslims. On this day, governed by a red star and the virtue of iron, let us pray for our Muslim brothers and sisters, warriors of God, consecrated to His grandeur so fully as to give their blood for Him, willing to give their lives for the principle that there is no other god but God. Lord, grant us their audacity and courage to confess our faith to the world, facing up to all dangers and consequences. Show them that the true holy war, as their prophet stated after battle, is the one which frees a man from within, overcoming hatred and avoiding the shedding of blood.

Tuesday. For the Tarahumara People. Let us pray for their strength and conviction. Do those who walk above, taking care of us, waver on their journey? Are those who provide Light to us up above lazy in their travels? Do those who watch over all of us from above ever rest? Let us pray for those celestial *raramuris* who are like our stars in the mountains, since each one of them, when they die, becomes one more star. Without them, all would be darkness in our nights. But let us also pray that those who are down here with us below will not abandon us during the day, despite their tremendous suffering and hunger. Let us pray that the Lord will help them to endure, to keep being the pillar of the world, to keep on sustaining the world.

✤ ✤ ✤

LUCAS DID NOT understand that mass very well. He had never imagined that someone from the Jesuit order could ever officiate and pray for students of mystery. But after that prayer Ketelsen opened his Bible and read the passage of the multiplying of the loaves and the fishes, and Lucas breathed more deeply. The commentary was especially moving:

"If we compare the two instances of multiplying narrated in the Gospel, we will note a curious difference. The first time there were five loaves, the multitude had 5000 people, and the number of baskets containing remaining fragments was twelve. The second time there were seven loaves, two more than the first; there were 4000 people, which was 1000 fewer; and the number of baskets was seven. With fewer loaves more people were filled and a greater amount was left over. When there are more loaves, fewer people are filled and a smaller amount of bread remains. What might be the moral meaning of this inverse proportion? That the less we have, the more we will be able to give away, just as we see in this privileged place in which we live. If the loaves had been even fewer, they would have filled twice the people, and the remaining fragments would have been even larger; this is what happens with us in this place as well. Less provides more: this is the miracle of poverty. Let us become united, here and now, by poverty. Imagine Jesus Christ taking poverty by the hand and telling us: 'Recognize this as your kingdom. Promise to pay it homage and fidelity.' It is so easy to say that poverty is a kind of shameful sickness, that no civilized, progressive nation deserves it, and that in the blink of an eye that scourge will be lifted from them. But the truth is that poverty, freely assumed, sanctifies. Not destitution, which is entirely different. Poverty is what we should imitate and choose, the product of voluntary renunciation, not of failure and impotence. For that reason I call you together here to sanctify our poverty, to see the San Sóstenes valley as a gift from God…"

Ketelsen's eloquence reverberated within the recently renovated walls of the church, reaching the altars and the art in the darkest recesses of the building. At times members of the heterogeneous congregation--almost the entire town was present--cleared their throats with disguised impatience, shifted on the hard wooden benches, and silenced any who made noises.

When Ketelsen held the host above his head, Lucas sensed an invisible presence he had not felt for many years. Right there. It was what he had futilely sought when he *nearly* fell from the bridge. It was an invisible presence but one that was more real, considerably more real than those temporary actors and that transitory theater.

When he took a portion of the host from the paten and placed it into his mouth, he had the clear sensation that if he spoke to Him, he would be heard.

He tapped his chest lightly with his fist, closed his eyes for a moment, and started to pray.

"Corpus domini nostri Jesuchristi."

As the host, that nearly illusory host, was disintegrating in his mouth, he asked: "Where am I, God, where am I? Give me a sign, I ask of Thee."

After the bread and wine had been administered, a sliver of smoke came out of the censer.

Contact with rays of the sun brought Lucas a measure of peace.

The Indians brought small animals, candles, and bundles of ocote wood for Ketelsen to bless. He opened the doors to the baptistery and, with Lucas at his side, spent several minutes disbursing torrents of holy water onto those fragile objects, investing in them supposed supernatural powers to conjure against the most varied of evils, and perhaps against Evil itself.

✤ ✤ ✤

AFTER HE FINISHED the blessings, Ketelsen went and sat on a small rock in the courtyard, surrounded by friends, Indians, infirm and children. He seemed jubilant and relaxed. Their conversations took on an intimate tone, their sentences a subtle structure, their questions an ambiguous, dense and sensitive flight. He lit up a cigarette. The light of the match lit up his pale face for a moment--his pupils projected intelligence and his jaw jutted out energetically.

At times Lucas had the impression that everyone present, even the children, had brief moments of inexplicable paralysis. It was as if for a few seconds everyone turned into statues at a wax museum, and only he could move about them and take it all in with his amazed eyes.

Tesgüino was recognized as a gift from *onnorúame* and therefore, when it was a part of a religious ceremony, they would first throw three small portions into the air. Next, whoever had prepared it would offer each container to the heads of the community for them to distribute in an orderly way.

Ketelsen took it and raised it above his head as if to elevate it to the stature of another holy host. He spoke as fluidly in Spanish as in Tarahumara. Lucas sensed enthusiasm (that word meaning God-inside, which he now kept ever present) in Ketelsen's transcending inward fire, in the contagious vibration of the words he said in response to the varied questions and commentaries people directed at him.

"I'm starting to see the face (which frankly was rather ugly) which I had in my prior life, just as you told me I would."

"Sometimes I sleepwalk and go to the cemetery unaware. When I open my eyes, upon finding myself among the crosses and the tombs I let out a shout and hurry home, running and stumbling. It happens more and more often."

"Last night I had a very strange dream which wasn't even my dream. I'm sure it wasn't mine. It came to me from some other place and from some other person. But where did it come from, and whose dream was it? Do you know, Father?"

"My sense of smell has become so heightened here that I can smell what they are cooking next door."

"The Tarahumaras say that one of these days a woman wearing a white shawl is going to come down here from a cave in the mountains and that three of us are going to die suddenly when she does. What do you know about this?"

"Sometimes it seems like I haven't returned from the hypnotic trance into which you placed me. It almost seems like I stayed over *there*. Perhaps you should snap your fingers in front of my face once again, but this time even louder."

"My deceased father was at my side yesterday as I went on a walk in the countryside. I could practically touch him. I sensed that if I reached out I actually would touch him. But that seemed to me to be an excess and a lack of faith at the same time. For the time being, we simply have long chats."

"From the time that you taught us to distinguish between pain and suffering (to isolate our pain in our bodies and keep it away from our minds), I deal much better with the colic which puts me onto the floor and ties me into knots after eating."

"How can I communicate with a sister I didn't say goodbye to before leaving my town?"

"Will you be at my side as I die, Father? Swear to it."

"Why is it that lately, when I close my eyes, when practically all I do is blink, the clear image of a cadaverous woman claiming to be my aunt comes to me?"

"Why did my pain suddenly shift to the other side of my body?"

"My adopted son can draw my dreams. He draws them better and better all the time. What a pity!"

"Does the euphoria that tesgüino produces come from God, Father? I ask because sometimes it creates inside of me almost a need to hit someone."

Ketelsen must have felt invisible to the world, and in a way he was, in that small valley, so small that it seemed more like the crater of a volcano covered with pine trees and surrounded by high mountains with enormous caves in which Indians lived. Sometimes, frequently, he lived in them also. Surrounded by peaks from which, miraculously, a small river of blue water descended, in that place Father Ketelsen could prove that death did not exist. It could only happen there. Where else? Aside from the train, and what a train it was, there was no other path to that refuge. Trying to scale the slopes leading up to it, as Lucas had found out, was nearly impossible. From a distance, from the surrounding mountains, from the air, from an airplane, no one would guess that the little valley existed.

Ketelsen said the following: "Let's suppose that from our world here above a visible light makes its way down to everyone 'down there.' A pure, visible light. What kind of transformation do you think there would be among people who are programmed, whether they recognize it or not, to accept nothing as reality unless they can touch it and see it? All you have to do is observe how people give themselves over to pleasure. They wouldn't do that, at least not to such excess, if they didn't see in pleasure a handhold saving them from nothingness, as a way to evade death. The truth is that if they were certain, absolutely certain, that they will keep living beyond the grave, they wouldn't be able to think about anything else, which is what we do. Pleasure would exist, but in a different, less vivid state, since its intensity is proportional to the attention we give it. It would pale like a kerosene lamp yielding to the light of the morning sun. Pleasure would be eclipsed by happiness…"

At that moment there came to Lucas, like a stab to his heart, the question that he had not wanted to ask, but which had constantly been on the tip of his tongue: How in the world was he going to get out of there?

Seeking some reassurance, Lucas whispered to Susila that he would need to leave the next day, somehow, please. His mother was very ill. He needed to go see her. He couldn't wait another day, not a single day.

"Fine," Susila answered calmly, "Mention to Ketelsen that you need to leave. It's no big deal."

Susila squeezed Lucas' hand and smiled at him. But it wasn't exactly a smile, but a gleam, something that did not come from any particular place and simply seemed to illuminate her, filling her face and body with light.

"I love you and I'm going to miss you down 'there,'" Lucas nearly told her, but he didn't dare.

TWENTY-SOMETHING YEARS OLD, his lanky, fragile body was sitting in his chair in such a way that it looked like he was about to fall. Joaquín's face was full of freckles and had a furrowed look, as if the sun were constantly hitting him in the face.

"One morning I was there, alone, just outside the laboratory, with the results of some exams in my hands. I remember night was approaching and I heard the sound of sparrows bidding farewell to the sun for the day from the tops of the trees. That farewell seemed as sad to me as my own personal situation. I walked a few blocks, thinking, meditating, calculating how I would break the news to my parents, to my sisters, to my teachers, and to my friends. Or would it be better to not tell them and flee my home, the city, the world? A friend of mine once told me that in Veracruz there is a place called Muro Norte, from which if a person jumps into the sea sharks eat him immediately, all at once, leaving no trace, as if he had never existed. The desolation of this world seemed to gradually grow as the sky filled with stars. But the bleakness of my soul surpassed that of the world to the extent that I felt sadness unlike anything I had ever felt, and which I hope to never feel again, for any reason. I would have cried if something inside me had been able to. I tried to pray, but failed at that as well. I sought the image of He in whom I believed, in whom I thought I believed, and an inner devastation was the response to my efforts. Without a doubt, He was not in me, but I wasn't even in me--I was somewhere else. I got onto the subway and that is where I met the man that told me about you. As I was turning my head toward the window our eyes met. He was several seats in front of me. You've probably seen how, in the darkness of the tunnels, the subway lights give a glow of quicksilver to our faces, they deform them, they make them look like plaster masks, but perhaps because of that they appear as they really are. His glance lighted upon mine like a beautiful bird and I smiled. It must have lasted for a moment or two, because I felt that the man had noticed my smile and he responded by inclining his head ever so slightly. He came over and sat by me and told me about you. He somehow managed to bring up the subject. He said that getting here was a complicated task, as it is hidden in the Tarahumara Mountains and very few people find it. But it existed, he was certain that it existed, even if other people denied it. He told me to look for it, to not give up, because if I really needed it, I would find it. And here you have me."

AFTER LUNCH, A frugal lunch consisting of dry meat, peaches, prickly pears, tea, and a pastry they prepared in their own ovens, they went out to take a walk. Ketelsen showed him with pride the little store to which anyone in town could go to get whatever they wanted without paying a cent. Did Lucas have any idea how many centuries of pain that region had suffered before this miracle came about? The doors on the entrance were open wide, while the back door, which led into a house, was half-closed. A plump woman with a round, happy face tended the store, sitting on a bench and covering a yawn with the back of her hand. There was a main counter, four shelves, and glass cabinets on the walls. Brown sugar, fragrant herbs, bags of dried meat, bottled fruits and honey, flour, cigarettes, jam, juices and soft drinks cooled by slabs of ice. Aspirin, suppositories, and some antibiotics. Candles hung from nails on the walls. They even gave away beer.

"The only thing we don't have is drugs. We run from peyote like the plague, we have all agreed. The only error Huxley committed, in my opinion, was to believe that we need drugs to open the doors of our perception. We have limited ourselves, as you have seen, to parapsychology, tesgüino, prayer, and manual labor, of course."

Ketelsen took some cigarettes and thanked the woman, who smiled, which rounded out even more fully her chubby face. What would happen if this were made known in other towns, in other parts of the mountains, in Creel, in La Junta, in San Juanito, Bocoyna or Madera? A *chabochi* would undoubtedly come, establish a pricing system, do some advertising, introduce canned and artificial foods, and start to offer products from other countries, since they sell so well.

"We have even saved some money from donations," added Ketelsen. "Some people want to give us more than we need and we prefer to take very little to have very little to store. It is better to avoid temptation, as the Lord's Prayer says. Whoever wants to can take some of our savings to visit the towns down below to buy whatever they may need. No one abuses the system."

"You are talking about a human condition which seems nothing like our own, father."

"We merely imitate the Tarahumaras. The sad thing is that no one has ever thought of adopting their moral code for use in their own community. We simply discovered what we had right under our noses."

"What do you sell down below?"

"Whatever we can, which isn't much. We sell a little here and a little there to keep the *chabochis* from paying too much attention to us. Wood, of course. Coal. But also woven blankets, bread, candles. Come see our candles."

A small group of men and women was in the middle of a courtyard under the sun. Wax was melting inside an enormous copper pot hanging over a fire. One person would hang a wick between two nails attached to turning wheels. Another would take melted wax from the pot and pour it over the strings. As the wheels would turn, the wax would form layers over the wick and the candles would take shape.

Ketelsen was taking very seriously the report Lucas was going to make to his superior, and he wanted to show him everything in great detail. A light fog made golden by the sun concealed potholes and loose rocks on the streets, where there was a smell of pine, bread, and recently cut wood. Ketelsen stopped to say hello to some men working with their water-carrying donkeys.

Other men were baking bread in an adobe oven. Spongy and covered with a light-brown crust, it came out of the oven smelling like holy bread, thought Lucas. They placed the loaves they were going to sell in baskets, arranging it so it wouldn't get damaged, and covering it with starched, white napkins.

Not far away some women were seated at a loom which extended like a small horizon. They passed the shuttles back and forth with precision and the designs were starting to take shape. Keep the string short to keep it tight to the shuttle, Ketelsen suggested to one of them, touching her hair gently.

He then led Lucas up a different path which wound through pine trees, then rice paddies, corn fields, terraced gardens--high up in the mountains!--fruit trees here and there, mounds cared for by the hands of laborers to protect the seeds hidden within, a system of irrigation. Lemon trees and peach trees. A peach tree in particular caught Lucas' eye--it had opened its flowering branches resulting in yellow and pink petals floating in the air with its sweet perfume. How could this area be so productive? Ketelsen simply winked in reply.

"It seems devilishly productive," said Lucas, and he was sorry the moment he said it.

"I have no doubt that he contributes. You know what a hard worker he is."

In a clearing in the forest, half a dozen provisional lumberjacks--some of our sick, Ketelsen affirmed--wearing just loincloths, were cutting off the branches of a recently felled tree. Controlling the cold and pain--not allowing it to reach the mind, in other words, not allowing it to become suffering--hunger, thirst and fatigue were some of the favored exercises of the community, something which awakened a bit of envy in Lucas. Hadn't he, during the first years of his religious training, practiced a bit of self flagellation along with a companion who had aspirations of sainthood? Just two sessions were enough for him to become thoroughly familiar with his body's indignant surprise. Rather than become humble, it seemed to growl at each lash.

"But come, Father Caraveo, we have to prepare for our attempt tonight to communicate with someone on the *other side* through one of our very sick patients who lives in a cave. You'll see."

Lucas stopped him, using his hand like a pincer on Ketelsen's forearm. He answered Lucas' worried look with a wry smile.

"Okay?"

"I have to leave tomorrow, father. Seriously. I won't be able to stay any longer."

"Of course! Go whenever you want" and he waved his hand. "Who is keeping you here? I'll be using hypnosis to operate on a cancerous tumor at noon. That may be of interest for your report. I would love to have you be there. Or you can leave before that. Don't forget that in this place, we all do whatever we want."

KETELSEN SAID: "ONE of those writers I read and re-read tells about an old man who wanted to die alone. Completely alone. He had always wanted that. He wanted to die with nobody at his side. He looked forward so much to death, and had done so for so long, that he didn't want to be taken by surprise, and so he prepared for it constantly, reverencing it. When he felt that his time was coming, he drove everyone out of the house with harsh shouting, forcing them out like unwelcome pests, so that he could receive death alone, to enjoy it as he wanted, to put into practice the reverential attitude that he had rehearsed for so long. That night, when he did indeed see death up close, his voice lost its vigor, but he dragged himself to the door with his eyes bulging, wanting to tell everyone about death. Her face was amazing. Contrary to what he had supposed, he just had to tell someone about it. That someone turned out to be a man who had entered his property to steal some oranges. That poor thief must have had the scare of his life. The dying man managed, half by threats and half by persuasion, to get him to stay and listen to him. After telling his story, he thanked the thief for listening and for watching him die, which brought him to his final breaths. Once he had told somebody, he died in peace. That is how we try to die here--we wait until we talk about death and say what we have to say."

As it was growing dark (in the mountains nightfall is preceded by a thick mist) animals were being led back from the countryside and men were returning from their work. A group of about a dozen men and three children went to the cave of the old man who was dying. They carried torches to light their way, as if in a religious procession. On the way they passed some goatherds, with whom someone in the group had a short conversation. They traveled quickly over slopes, around bushes, and under trees. Ketelsen was particularly nimble--like a monkey, and never shed a drop of sweat. They saw the luminous pupils of owls, heard various animal calls, including the exasperated melodies of crickets, felt things brush furtively on their skin and other things poke them like needles, stepped on tender plants that groaned and on dry leaves that whispered as they disintegrated under foot. They climbed to the top of a hill and descended to the bottom of a ravine.

At one point Lucas slipped, sending a rock off the path and down into the mystery of the abyss. He stood paralyzed, staring downward and shivered at the thought that he very nearly fell.

"Leave it alone. Don't obsess with what is down there, as the Tarahumaras say. Instead look up. Look, rain is about to catch us," said Ketelsen, who was walking at his side with one of the torches.

Clouds were descending onto the mountains. They were dark and sticky. From time to time a flash of lightning would theatrically illuminate the beautiful mountainside, and a few seconds later the distant and intermittent rattling of thunder would follow. A light rain occasionally fell on them, which the children quite enjoyed, and they had to go a stretch without torches, covering their heads with blankets and jackets. But their pace never slackened. Every so often a small gust of wind would dislodge a few drops of rainwater from the leaves of the trees.

As they turned because of a small stream, they saw the place: a cliff with three vertical rises, and at the foot of the second there was a very round and dark eye of a cave.

"There it is."

There was an opening about a meter in diameter which two oak trees, clinging to the rocks, made almost invisible. A torch hung from the rock illuminated the cave which had a high ceiling and a floor of dry sand. It was cold, as if fit for a bear. A stench hit Lucas, and he decided to linger near the cave's entrance.

Stretched out on a mat there was a man covered by a fraying blanket. His bloodshot eyes shone from within the protruding orbits of his bony face. His hair was like the plumage of a bird which just died. "A countenance flayed by regret so profound that it would embarrass whoever might be capable of laying eyes upon it," thought Lucas, unable to remember where he had read that.

The man's eyes grew humid and he lifted a wrinkled hand when he saw Ketelsen, who sat on the floor next to him in the half lotus position, and spoke to him in Tarahumara. There was a group of Indians around the man. The men were barefoot and wore mended clothes, and the women wore shawls and colorful kerchiefs around their heads.

Ketelsen asked all who were present, even the children, to sit in the same position he was in, but several people struggled and found it to be impossible even with help. He told them to hold hands and to not let go for any reason, please, because if the chain was broken it could cause damage. (He whispered to Lucas that one time they let go and his nose started to bleed profusely.) A candle was burning near the face of the dying man, which gave him a perfectly monstrous look. Lucas felt Ketelsen's hand become tense as he held it. On the other side of the circle, an Indian woman's hand reminded him of a fish out of water.

Ketelsen recited several names in Tarahumara and the sick man responded. Suddenly Ketelsen started to breathe deeply which soon became a roaring death rattle, exactly the sound of a man in intense agony. At times he flung his head so far back that it looked like it was about to tumble off, or he shook it like a dog coming out of water. His hand tightened onto Lucas' hand, his fingernails digging into it.

On the roof of the cave a subtle phosphorescence started to appear. (The sky looks that way when the night begins its arrival, thought Lucas, when the stars start to amalgamate, yielding to some sort of plotting, hostile pressure, resisting their re-encounter, their constellations, opposing eyes that search for them and attract them, overcoming their velvety unreachability, until they appear ten at a time at first, then by the hundred, all within the sight of a single person.) The phosphorescence gave way to tiny spheres that started to burst, one after another, pop, pop, pop. Sometimes they gave off pale, cool light, like fireflies. White, yellow, or slightly violet. They had a more intensely luminous nucleus, like a little spark. Ketelsen explained to him later that those little spheres, closely related to the spectral lights, were partial materializations.

But the actual materialization began with a gold powder-like substance that the little lights left on the floor, or just above the floor, near the dying man. From its midst, in a luminous explosion, a column of white smoke appeared and then became a body. It was an Indian like any of the men in attendance, but enveloped in a tunic-like ozone cloud. Lucas could distinguish even the wrinkles on his face and the turn of his mouth. His hands would intermittently become transparent depending on the fluctuations of the ozone from white to greenish. He reached down to stroke the forehead of the dying man. Several participants in the circle, undoubtedly relatives of the man, cried and spoke to him in loud voices. The children's eyes were as big as saucers.

Despite his surprise, it occurred to Lucas that this was all just an issue of light (Light), which brought order to chaos, transformed the unreal into reality, and made visible what is constantly present but which we do not see. As in any fortuitous encounter of favorable elements, all that was needed was for light to invade the niches, seemingly cold and austere spaces, corners, caves such as this one, for a tremor of life to be made manifest and transform everything in its timeless and spaceless dance. Ketelsen was simply attracting and freezing light into a precious, palpable, autonomous substance. Or was it exactly the opposite? Autonomous? It had to do with objects which were solid and movable, which expanded in light and color, which trembled in space, but their hearts would only beat when called upon by an outer source. Lucas decided that it wouldn't do him any harm to read some books dealing with the occult.

That night, in honor of the fleeting and luminous apparition of their deceased relative and the subsequent improvement in morale of the sick man, the Indians held an impromptu celebration outside the cave from which Lucas and Ketelsen were unable to escape. Lucas had to eat several portions of popcorn to ameliorate the tesgüino. He was told to eat popcorn to be able to keep on drinking tesgüino. That night happiness took on the body of a god that danced in the midst of a hundred bright mirrors and a hundred iridescent lights, which would not disappear from Lucas' view no matter how often he blinked, to the sound of wild maracas and energized drums.

In spite of the frigid wind which removed him from time to time from the rhythm of the celebration, swallowing up the lights and erasing the sounds, the effect of the tesgüino and a thick blanket they lent him allowed him to stay on his feet nearly until dawn.

When they returned, as they maneuvered past the hills and the constant chasms, Ketelsen spoke to him with a vehemence exceeding any other he had shown to that point. He began with a confession:

"Susila is right. I can't handle tesgüino as well as I used to."

"I HAD A dream saturated in boredom which caused my insanity, and my insanity drove me to the brink of death and brought me here." Paco's face had sharp features, a small moustache, and was very serious, although small bursts of a clucking laughter emerged from time to time from behind his teeth and lips. "'San Sóstenes is kind of an insane asylum where, perhaps, you will be able to wake up.' That's what my doctor told me who recommended that I come and join you here, and he was right. I wasn't actually entirely insane, at least so my doctor and I figure; I simply took a hard look at insanity, as if looking into an aquarium where an octopus creates, then half-awake destroys the vague clouds of a nightmare. Am I making sense? Those of us who are not entirely insane, as I suppose was my case, scarcely perceive a gust of that unbreathable air, and the door opens up, letting in a ray of light which drives away those murmurs from the 'other' world (so close to ours that we can almost see it as we blink) like frightened spiders. What must it be like to go there permanently? All I have to do is think about it (given my background) and I get goose bumps. It has always amazed me that the mechanism of dreams, any dream, must obey the laws of wakefulness, which are then overruled a few hours later by another dream. It seems like a supreme violation of the minimal daytime rules of reason. Given the conduct of some who are insane, and the assurance and faith that is evident in all they say and do, and their unrestrained anger due to our inability to understand them, I decided that perhaps insanity comes from transporting a dream, any dream, from one side to the other, from which a man or child would never awake. I came very close to having that happen to me and I knock on wood to keep it from happening to me," and he did indeed knock on the leg of the chair he was using. "A dream that invades and replaces wakefulness, like what happens with delirium, hope, faith or love. Our souls go off to a different place, as the Tarahumaras would say. That is why a simple phrase Father Ketelsen read to me here affected me so profoundly: 'Insanity is a dream that doesn't end.' My dream repeated itself over and over without any variations, and as time went on I had it with greater frequency: I was standing for hours and hours (which in a dream could well have been just one second) in front of a simple chess set. If a person is not at all interested in chess (as was the case for me), it is insufferable to be stuck looking at a game of it that was started who knows when and by who knows who. I had that dream so much that a huge sadness enveloped me, they admitted me into a clinic, and my spirit became incapable of dealing with the faces which came into contact with me--they became equivalent to chess pieces. Each morning I would awaken groaning, convulsively shaking my hands and feet, and suddenly a totally negative shout would erupt from inside of me, emanating from my entire body, a rejection of whatever was seeping into me--practically a sticky substance--during my dream. I found very little pleasure in the flavor of food or in seeing something beautiful--it was miserly pleasure. My pleasure was strictly self-centered. At some point I started to pray: 'I don't know what to do, Lord, and even the echo of my own, poor pleasure makes me tired!' To wake up from my dream, the doctor who sent me here told me I needed something drastic, like a floodlight from a guard tower, or a moment of clarity like poets, believers, lovers, and travelers experience. He said that those people never get tired of gazing on the faces of people around them. There are people who are practically ablaze, he assured me, who light up people who see them. Those are the faces I came in search of here."

✣ ✣ ✣

AFTER RETURNING FROM the cave, with dawn almost upon them, Ketelsen's laugh and the breeze shivered, broke off, and then mixed together. He slapped Lucas on the back with an unnecessary roughness and questioned the need for the report he was preparing for his superior.

"What could today's Church possibly understand about this place? What? Why don't you instead stay here and live with us," Lucas almost tripped and fell at the suggestion, "so that you can have what we have-- an alternative for people who refuse to yield to the claws of fatality."

Lucas replied that he had to deliver his report, that the principle of obedience demanded it of him. Ketelsen proposed that they do a little summary together. Lucas heard Ketelsen's voice echo, bouncing off the high walls of the mountains, which the morning fog had made almost invisible. Ketelsen asked Lucas to guess, based on what they could see from that spot--with the fog in the way?--how much work it had taken for this land to become fruitful.

"Consider the planning and digging of impossible canals that it would seem only the devil could have built. You've seen them. Think about plowing up and cultivating this rocky ground and getting it to produce corn, rice, beans, prickly pears, lemons and peaches. Think about what is involved in raising goats and getting them to multiply. This work was all done shoulder to shoulder with the Indians. It was a labor of faith--faith above all else--to make these fields and stockyards what they are today. It was all so that people could be together and die in the fullness that you have witnessed. And all this for what?"

He heaved a prolonged sigh, then gulped down a large mouthful of the mist.

"So that San Sóstenes, at the proper moment, will satisfy the dreams of *everyone* who is *down there.* Some day everyone will know about her domes and towers beneath a sky as resplendent and shining as the smile of a woman in love. As roses are to flowers and gold is to metals, that is how San Sóstenes will be to those who arrive here--they won't be able to resist coming--to confirm that it actually exists."

The tesgüino did go to his head, confirmed Lucas.

"A bigger and bigger throng of people, peaceful and rejoicing, will fill her streets. Exiles will return here to the land of their birth. No one will judge anyone else. There will be no politicians, law enforcement personnel, bankers, business people, thieves, prostitutes or children starving to death."

They were going downhill, the rain had erased the supposed trail, and the ground was loose, so they had to be careful with each step to avoid taking a tumble. Lucas decided to grab Ketelsen's robe to force him to slow down, to put the brakes on his wild rush, to keep from breaking a leg. That's all he would have needed in that barren wasteland where there wasn't even a bird overhead to make him feel like less of an orphan. And it was at that spot, at that hour, that it occurred to Ketelsen to speak about his megalomaniacal dreams?

"Everything is so simple that they will simply end up opening their eyes. Certainly the morality of the world is in a sickly state, but it isn't incurable. Even we were confused and dazed by the cataclysms of the empire of death under which we had been living. Nevertheless, wasn't it conceivable that the validity of its inflexible structure would slowly start into decline? And isn't it likely that such a change would create room for creative, unheralded possibilities, for utopian endeavors, even within disaster itself? It became very clear that when death has chosen someone, that person discovers this truth: that at the very end, death is no longer horrible, because death is the opposite of horror. Yes, I have seen many people try to run from death, terrified by her, frightened by her inevitable arrival, but don't kid yourself, Lucas, I've never seen anyone in a state of fright who is truly dying."

This was the first time he called Lucas by his first name (he wasn't sure how he felt about this). He then offered Lucas a confession which, instead of calming his concerns, confirmed them:

"I, personally, will never grow tired of transmuting."

✠ ✠ ✠

STOUT, WITH A thick neck and a ruddy complexion, Emilio seemed exhausted as he sat in his chair, and shook his head to emphasize his words.

"I had been suffering various aches and pains, but I tried to ignore them. I walked up and down the stairs with my body like a limp rag. Several years prior I stopped smoking, but I had smoked two to three packs a day my entire life. Suddenly something snapped inside of me, like a tense cord that reaches its limit. I remember finding myself on a gurney rushing down a frozen hallway in a hospital, wanting only to be asleep or anesthetized. I felt clearly being taken from the gurney and placed on an operating table and I felt a woman's hands cradling my head. I also remember they put a small white cart next to me, and that a blonde nurse rubbed alcohol onto my arm then pricked me with a needle which connected to a tube attached to a bottle full of a milky liquid. A very old man dressed in white came with an apparatus made out of metal and leather which he put on my arm to check something. Another man wearing a mask and amber gloves so tight that his hands looked like those of a cadaver signaled to someone who was standing behind me. I'm telling you all these details because suddenly, I saw myself from the highest part of the room, my body stretched out on the operating table, with physicians trying to revive me, causing horrible convulsions--which I thought I could feel, but actually I couldn't--until I heard one of the doctors say 'There's nothing we can do. He's gone.'

I heard that clear as day. I heard it and then I kept hearing it in my dreams, in all of the dreams I had in the subsequent days, when I had been revived: 'There's nothing we can do. He's gone.'"

As Emilio said that, his neck became even broader and his voice trembled and became prickly.

"This resurrection has not been easy. I've become familiar with a state of the soul which does not correspond to this life, but isn't death either, but a sort of confusing borderland between the two. I have been existing between two nights--the night below, the world which I have been in the process of abandoning, whose forms, colors, and sounds seem more and more distant, and the night above--the one off which I can't take my eyes. I thank God for giving me a little more time--I had plenty of debts to settle--but I can't help looking up constantly. It is as if my soul has bitten an invisible hook used by an invisible fisher who is pulling from above."

THE ACT OF opening his eyes was once again nearly fatal. What he had just experienced came alive again in his dreams. They were so intensely clear and painful that it woke him violently numerous times. His memory was full of truncated images and disjointed voices. "I am mortal, I am mortal, I am mortal." The only thing that seemed alive in his little room was a narrow ray of light coming through the window and another thicker one which landed on his blanket. The bed's sheets were rough, but fresh, and had the smell of a fruit which he couldn't identify.

He thought: "I have to get out of here today. I have to leave this place today, and I haven't started the report for my superior. I should do it while what I've seen and heard, which has been considerable, is still fresh in my mind." But Lucas felt a vivid reaction against the act of writing--he felt that the act of writing itself would be impossible. In the distant past, when he had first entered the order, he wrote something every day. He believed that his writing would be able to help save souls, even if it was just a few chosen souls. He thought that some day, in due time, he would publish something, why not? But when he showed his notebook to a superior, the subsequent eyebrow raisings spoke volumes more than the commentaries which came immediately after, and Lucas recognized the error of his thinking. And now this. What is this? What is it all about, exactly? Perverse utopias, unprecedented worlds, places that cannot exist, promises of impossible human happiness, deceitful appearances destined to create unreachable illusions in gullible readers. Please, Father Caraveo, we live in a valley of tears, and you need to get used to that idea. In his mind's eye, he saw page after page of small letters blackened and bursting into providential flames because they were condemned to that fate moments before by their own creator. And that would be the best possible outcome.

He had the sensation that his body was slighter than before, lost under the sheets, and with his hands folded on his chest like a statue of stone at a sepulcher. It was as if he was preparing for whatever could happen. He breathed rhythmically, squeezing his knees together slightly. He started to pray, although he didn't really want to, so it took great effort:

"Hail Mary, full of grace, the Lord be with thee, blessed art thou among women..."

But he couldn't go on, and he wasn't sure why--at that hour of the day and as tired as he was, he started to cry. But the sound of it didn't seem to alter the silence that surrounded him, profound and fierce, like the silence of sleeping beasts. It was almost a calming cry, repeating the same tone, like a child practicing over and over again the pronunciation of a vowel in a foreign language. It was, come to think of it, like the Tarahumara children who practiced a foreign language in that strange place.

SUSILA PREPARED A caesalpinia flower tea for him, ideal for a hangover, and she explained that his recent cogitations and fears were the product of tesgüino, without a doubt. She said that happened especially to people unaccustomed to drinking tesgüino, but within a few minutes he would be just fine because of the tea. It seemed to be specially made by the hand of God for those who drink tesgüino. She said that in the afternoon she would give him another root to reinforce the treatment, but that in the meantime he was to eat very little and avoid fat, if possible.

They were seated on the edge of the bed and Susila was smiling at him with her eyes. Lucas was shaking, he had shivers, and his voice sounded odd, as if there were a hole in the middle of each word.

"Do you remember when I arrived and I told you about the bridge?"

"I remember it well."

"There was nothing beneath it," and a bitter taste invaded his mouth.

"You didn't see anything," her thick mouth stretched out, tenderly, with a weak vibration which seemed to echo the rhythm of his blood.

"Nevertheless, during mass, for a moment there was something… Do you understand?" and he left his lips rounded, as if keeping back one last phrase.

"Give me your hand."

Susila took one of his hands into hers and stroked gently the palm and then the back of his hand, following the sinuous veins, and it gave him goose bumps. Lucas felt a surge of boiling blood which ran up to his face. She seemed to attract *that* simply with her touch, seemed to make it visible to him, make it come alive. So many other times he felt terror but for no particular reason, on entirely forgettable days, or perhaps it stemmed from some cause too old for him to remember, which was suppressed inside of him.

"Go ahead and express what you are feeling."

Then Lucas felt like he really was falling. Not like at the bridge--which he could now see was a purely mental phenomenon--but this time he was really falling. He embraced her and kissed her gently on her neck. He was deeply affected by her warm skin and it caused a sensation deep inside his chest, a confused desire, which ended up causing him to tighten his hands into fists. Might this be part of the tesgüino experience? "Let yourself go," she told him, egging him on, openly encouraging him. "Let go of everything. I've been telling you to do that since the night you arrived."

Lucas finally wept with tangible tears--silver reflections descended irrepressibly down his cheeks. He fiercely tried to dry them with his hands until she gave him a handkerchief. He stammered and stuttered, complaining about his bad luck and misfortunes. And then he erupted, amid sobs and tears, and he spewed his bitterness and desperation, past and present, his wasted youth, his frustration with life and the priesthood. He spoke with a sincerity that he had never shown even to himself. He told her how miserable and forlorn he felt for never having shared a great love--that he feared nothing more than a possible sexual relationship--for not becoming the successful writer he thought he would become, and for knowing that he was going to die right there even more stupidly than he had lived. He said he had even practiced saying: "My name is Lucas and I'm going to die..." He asked if she wanted to know his real problem, then realized that of course she already knew it, since she could read minds. He said that his real problem was that he wasn't like them—they were free from ambition, plans, doubts and prejudices, they were always even-tempered, connected to other people, and resigned and ready at whatever moment for death. He was like the people down there, and he nearly put his finger through the mattress as he said it. That is why he should go away that day at the latest. Could she help him?

Susila took his face between her hands, gently squeezing his cheeks, and said very seriously:

"I can't. Only Ketelsen can. Do you understand?"

"Yes, I understand. That train..., I can't take it, can I?"

Susila shook her head, no.

✛ ✛ ✛

"BUT DON'T BE so solemn, man of God." And she invited him to visit a sick, dying old woman to cheer him up and round out his report to his superior.

"Another?" Lucas asked, and his shoulders drooped. "You've seen how I'm not like you in the way you lift your spirits by visiting people who are dying. I'm envious."

But this individual was very different because she was as peaceful and resigned as was possible. Susila invited him to come and see for himself.

"Can you guarantee that we won't have to drink tesgüino if she gets better?"

The sun was directly overhead. How many hours must I have slept, he wondered. It was a sun that would touch the roofs of the houses, then permeate them pleasantly.

On the way Lucas asked: "Do you say something special to people who are dying? ...if you don't mind me asking."

"I help them to keep practicing the art of living, even when they are in pain. I help them to know who they truly are. These are the only things that can really help dying people to continue to the end. And perhaps beyond the end."

"In other words, you try to help them to recognize their identity even in their final moments."

"From the beginning to the end, anguish is the loss of one's true identity. You know that better than anyone."

Lucas was going to follow up on that topic, but at that moment they arrived at a home which had been adapted to be like a small hospital, where they were told that the sick woman had taken a very grave turn for the worse. They hurried into a large, well lit room with a line of beds separated by folding screens. In contrast to the hospitals "down there," the nurses here--most of whom were simply inhabitants of the town--did not wear white and did not have pedantic attitudes of self sufficiency. With the exception of intravenous drips, the sick were not tethered to sophisticated machines. And the most important difference was the absence of the feeling--the aura--of anguish and tragedy that dominates down there. The gravely or terminally ill had company that had been specially trained to take care of them. And if they were there, in that hidden spot in the Tarahumara Mountains, it was because they were resigned to die, without a doubt.

The old woman's jaw seemed to nearly come out of joint from the effort she gave to take in air, and her eyes were riveted upward. Her arms were mere bones covered by dry and wrinkled skin, and her hands were like claws. Here we go again with the Essential Horror of the final days, thought Lucas, when will it end? A nurse stood and offered her seat to Susila, on one side of the bed. Lucas remained standing on the other side. Rays of sunshine were coming through the partially closed curtains.

"Wake up, Elena!" Susila said as she arrived, adding a pat on her shoulder. "Don't go to sleep. It's not time yet. Wake up, Elena!"

This seemed to Lucas a cruel way to treat the poor dying woman, since he had been told that she had already received her last communion from Ketelsen. But he decided that he should not intervene as it was a special situation between two women. And after all, they were in the valley of San Sóstenes.

"I wasn't really sleeping," she replied, "it's just that I am very weak, very weak. It seems like every time I close my eyes I'm about to go through the eye of a needle."

"But you have to be here. Up! You have to know that you are here." Susila slipped another pillow under the head of the sick woman and gave her a bit of water, which looked iridescent in that light. "Is the pain very intense?"

"It would be," she replied in a mere thread of a voice, "if it truly were my pain. But, who knows why, but it isn't mine any more. The pain is real, but distant. Maybe I am starting to be over there, with them…"

"Not yet. Until the proper moment you need to stay here. Here and now until the end, as conscious of yourself as is possible. It will be a lot easier than if you sleep, believe me."

"Tell me something to help me keep my eyes open, Susila, please."

Lucas thought about the number of sleeping pills and painkillers they would have given to this woman "down there," in addition to connecting her to all sorts of machines. Was this truly better? Susila breathed profoundly, as if she were about to go under water.

"Let's see. Nothing confusing. Just the straightforward reality of dying in simplicity. What else was there? But be careful of the shifting sands that try to bury you in fear, in self-pity, and desperation. So walk smoothly, Elena. Stand on your tiptoes, if that's possible, and don't take any baggage, not even a carry-on bag. Don't take anything… Leave it all behind. You're not taking anything, are you?"

"Nothing," the woman answered, her eyes dark and round like rubber balls, fixed on a point on the ceiling. Death is right there, thought Lucas. If I were to look into the depths of her eyes, I would see it clearly.

"No guilt or regrets," said Susila.

"Nothing"

A moment later the old woman seemed to give up, to discontinue her superhuman effort--which it truly was--and she closed her eyes. Finally, thought Lucas, and he started to breath more smoothly.

"I'm going to sleep, Susila. I can't go on any longer. But keep talking to me, please."

Susila kept talking to her in hushed tones, next to her ear, with her sweet, suggestive, melodious voice. Just from what he managed to hear, Lucas felt that his legs were losing their strength, and he looked around for a vacant chair, but couldn't find one. He shuddered at the thought of collapsing at the moment of the woman's death. But it was truly as if Susila's voice possessed a power that could enchant anyone.

"You are floating in that great, calm, silent river that flows with such serenity that you could almost think the water is asleep. A sleeping river. But it flows inexorably. Life flows silently and irresistibly toward a living peace, so much deeper, so much richer and more powerful for people who know its pains and sorrows, for people who know them and welcome them and convert them into a different substance. You are floating toward that peace right now, Elena, floating in that calm, silent river which is sleeping and is irresistible. I am floating with you. We're traveling together. It doesn't take any effort on our part at all. I'm with you. We don't have to do anything or think anything. I'm letting go with you, letting myself be carried along as well. Let's ask this irresistible sleeping river of life to carry us where it is going... And we know that where it is going is where we want to go, where we should go. Down the sleeping river toward complete reconciliation..."

The woman puffed with a scratchy sound. She tried to say something, but was unable.

"Fall asleep in the sleeping river," Susila continued. "Above the river the sky is pale and there are white clouds. When you look at them, you start to float toward them. Yes, float upwards. The river is now a river in the air, an invisible river which takes us ever upward. We leave the hot plains and move toward the freshness of the mountains. The cool air is so pleasant--fresh and pure, full of life."

The woman was gasping mouthfuls of air which she could no longer swallow. The cry of a newborn and the rattle of the dying, thought Lucas.

"You can now let go, my friend," she ran her hand through the woman's grey hair with long undulating strokes. "Leave this poor, old body behind. You don't need it any more. Be free of it. Let go now, let go of everything. Leave this worn out body here and go forward. Go on, go toward the light, toward peace, toward the living peace of the clear light."

Finally, Susila took one of the lifeless hands of the old woman and kissed it.

"The time has come for us to go," she said.

Lucas asked to stay a moment longer to say a prayer.

The woman had slowly been shrinking, noticeably sinking down into the bed to the point that she almost disappeared into it. She curled up as if to facilitate her passage to the cemetery, which was actually more like a common burial ground, given the crowded geometry of anonymous graves. There were more graves than houses in the town. If people came there to die they had to be buried somewhere. The crosses were very simple, unornamented, barely two sticks of wood without any inscription. Susila told Lucas that it was better that way. They simply placed the naked body of the old woman into a hole, placed dirt onto her, made a little hill which they covered with rocks, and Ketelsen pronounced some simple words. Perhaps it was there, at that moment, that the dark cloud which had been following Lucas disappeared for an instant. It was an instant he could not prolong. He saw something from the other side (that is, from this side). It was like figures of a final accounting, figures brought into balance without words or actions: a simple realization of truly falling into the abyss.

HE WAS A young Indian with a robust complexion. He was wearing rough clothing and work boots.

"I'm going to tell you about him, like I promised. The women sat down on a stone wall and the men, we kept on standing. We were next to the mouth of the cave, all of us looking at him, the man who had just died. We all knew that he was going to die, since he had announced it, but none of us thought that he would do it the way he did. It made us all angry. The *sipame* sat on a rock next to the feet of the dead man. He took the flower out of his hair and started to shake him up and down and from side to side, through the power of his thought processes, so that the dead man would hear his words better. 'Why are you here,' he asked. And the dead man answered clear as day. We all heard him: 'Because I'm dead. Can't you see me?' 'Why are you dead?' 'Because I died, like I said.' 'But why did you die?' 'Because I decided to.' 'Why did you decide to die?' 'Because I got tired of living.' 'That's not good--aren't you ashamed?' No response, so the *sipame* insisted: 'Tell me, why did you hang yourself from that tree?' 'Because I felt like it, that's why.' 'And what have you gained by it, since before long you'll just be buried under a mound of rocks?' 'I'm happy, like I never was on that side.' 'Yes, but what about your family, your animals, and all of us?' 'I don't care; I wanted to be happy over here.' 'Don't come back to us. Do you hear me? We don't want to see you any more. That's why we're going to burn your body. We aren't going to bury you--we're going to burn you instead.' Before she

94

left, his wife went over to the dead man and said, practically spitting it out at him: 'You good for nothing! You've abandoned us!' Then we all went to a well where we soaked our clothes and everything to erase any contact our bodies might have had with the dead man, and when we went home we changed out of them. That night we had a very good celebration. We surrounded a large fire that threw its light onto the large old pine trees. We asked everybody and decided that it was better to burn the dead man's body than to bury it. After we had heard his words we were afraid that his soul would return to take someone else with him. We didn't want his ideas to affect anyone else. That happens sometimes. That's the good thing about asking recently deceased people what they want and why they did what they did, the *sipame* told me. His wife also said that she thought it would be better to burn him."

"THERE ISN'T TO be any pain--none," Ketelsen ordered, with a voice so sharp that it seemed like a scalpel already in the sick man's body. The man's face was deformed, swollen due to an enormous abscess in his gums, and there was an anguish centered in his eyes which were like those of animals in flight.

The large white room had cracks in the walls and the floor was chipped but it was obviously clean and freshly painted. On one side of the bed's headboard was a small wooden table with blue and red bottles, containers of gauze and cotton, probes, and a pair of scalpels wrapped in a flaxen cloth. There was an open bottle of water with some bubbles in it which reflected a bluish hue from the window. Outside, the afternoon sun highlighted the mountains. Indian women were getting water from a nearby well.

Ketelsen's fingers ran over the body of the sick man as if they were playing an invisible piano. They went from the crown of his head along his face and chest to his upper stomach. The man's muscles clearly relaxed. A nurse seated to his side dried the sweat from his brow. Sixty, eighty, one hundred, one hundred twenty more strokes and it seemed like the piano was slightly extending its imaginary keyboard with each stroke.

"Sometimes it takes more than an hour to get them completely to sleep, and you can never be sure that they are one hundred percent asleep," Ketelsen explained to Lucas. "A couple of my patients woke up in the middle of an operation (a truly horrible thing), but it's better to take that risk in this kind of difficult case, because it is quite probable that he wouldn't survive the use of Pentothal."

"This is his last chance," thought Lucas, and in a place like San Sóstenes, for Heaven's sake. Surely the sick man knew there was no hope--that was their huge advantage here--and so he had made his home on this *other side*, far away, irreparably far away, no matter the outcome of the operation.

How *far* was it, really?

The sick man started to sink slowly into his pillow. He also began to snore, quietly, in small whistling sounds, at a regular pace.

About an hour later, Ketelsen was exhausted. He paused, opened and closed his hands as if squeezing lemons, dried off his face with a towel from the nurse, went over to the window for some air, then took a couple of puffs on a cigarette. He then sat next to the bed, took one of the sick man's hands, and checked his pulse.

"See that? Just a little while ago it was a hundred. Now it is seventy."

He lifted the man's arm, and his hand dangled lifelessly. He asked the nurse to do the same with the other arm, with the same result. When she let go, his hand fell with a thud. Look at this, Father Caraveo. Pay attention, Father Caraveo. It bothered Lucas that they seemed to assume that he was familiar with this type of procedure. It was actually all he could do to keep standing, since his legs were becoming wobbly.

"Everything's ready. Let's begin."

Ketelsen started to explore the tumor, and beckoned Lucas to come closer. Its roots were in the man's jawbone, but it had spread out and had almost filled his nose. "Look at this, Father, it has reached the socket of his right eye, and is starting to obstruct his throat."

Ketelsen carefully washed his hands up to his wrists with cotton soaked in alcohol, then washed up again after putting on some tight, amber-colored latex gloves. When he took one of the scalpels out of the cloth, there was a tiny metallic sound which seemed piercing to Lucas.

Ketelsen told the nurse that, just in case, she should have the probe ready to go into the internal ear through his nasal passages, and if necessary, into the occipital cranial cavities. He then described to Lucas and the nurse, step by step, what he was doing.

"I begin by tightening his skin," and he pulled the skin tight and cut into the man's cheek with the scalpel. "I make a small incision here. I cut the underlying connective tissue. I open up his cheek all the way to his nose. From time to time I pause to tie off blood vessels... Are you following me?"

Lucas started to feel queasy, but it somehow didn't seem right to ask--at a moment such as that--to pull up a chair and sit down, as if he were watching some kind of variety show, or to stop looking at the face undergoing an operation. It seemed as though he was looking at that face at the bottom of a well. While he was studying at the Regional Institute of Chihuahua with the Jesuits, on one occasion he flatly refused to attend the biology class in which they were going to dissect a rabbit to study its anatomy. His teacher understood--several students felt the same way--and it didn't affect his final grade. Good heavens! And now he was supposed to witness an entire surgical procedure with a patient anesthetized through hypnosis and who could wake up at any moment, as Ketelsen himself had admitted? If that were to happen, how would the man raise his bloody face from the pillow? What kind of a shriek would he emit? And the question that had gnawed at Lucas constantly these days came back more pressingly than ever: what the devil was he doing there?

When the queasiness became more pronounced, he looked up at the ceiling and only occasionally, out of the corner of his eye, did he look at the swollen face, which seemed to have turned into a piece of candy, into a bloody pudding of skin, bones, teeth and hair all mixed around. The gauze was avidly absorbing blood. "Look! Look, Father Caraveo." Every so often the nurse would raise the sick man's head to let him cough and spit the blood that had accumulated in his trachea into a bowl. Ketelsen proudly commented: "Look, Father, not even this wakes him up."

And then he announced loudly: "Let's finish up!"

Lucas couldn't help but look down, and that was his mistake. At that moment Ketelsen introduced his fingers into the throat of the patient, and then pulled them out with the root of the tumor. It looked like a small green toad about to jump. Lucas felt that he was drowning in a small, black empty space, and he fainted.

"MY NAME IS Laura and I'm going to die," she was twenty-something years old and had a delicate, graceful appearance. "Or rather, someone else already died in my place, and his final wish was for me to come and tell you about it. It started when a very rare illness attacked me--a virus in my heart, which is very serious. I started to feel nausea, palpitations, tachycardia, shortness of breath, a lump in my throat.

They took me to a hospital and hooked me up to electrodes, suction, and probes. On a television to which I was connected I could see the wavy lines and intermittent stars which my feeble heart produced. That was my situation when a friend of mine bought me a very special book, which cured me. The more I read the more comprehensible my sudden recuperation seemed. And why not, I told myself, since each time I turned a page I felt an abundance of enthusiasm, a certain passage brought my blood pressure back to normal, my heart was beating rhythmically by the book's final lines, and my blood flowed as smoothly as its musical prose. The virus vanished to the astonishment of the physicians. A few days later my friend visited me at my home. I told him the book he had given me had cured me. 'I started to read it and from the very beginning I started to feel better. The doctors can't believe it. They say no one is cured just by reading a book. Did you read it?' He said that he had not read it, that he had bought it for me on a recommendation, but that no, he hadn't read it. I asked him how he could give a book as a gift which he hadn't read. He said that someone had recommended it especially for me. It was someone from here, from this part of the Tarahumara Mountains, but he never saw that person again and couldn't even remember his name. Just read the book today and you'll see. We agreed to come here to be with you, to say thanks, almost like a pilgrimage. Except that he read the book that same night and the next day a virus attacked his heart, and he never recovered from it. I visited him in the hospital, and he was connected to that same television which showed the wavy lines and intermittent stars which his infirmed heart produced. Before he died he made me promise to come here to tell you what happened. And so he and I could be reunited here."

WHEN HE FIRST awoke, it was total confusion. All of the sensations which had been dulled came rushing back to him, and he tried to somehow forget that horrid image of a frog emerging from a bleeding neck poised to leap onto him. He gasped for air, searching for some relief in his lungs. His hands opened and closed in a void that was black once again. He found it difficult to keep his eyes open. His drowsiness was stronger than he was. But each time his eyes closed, he would immediately see the image of the frog and would sit up, terrified, in bed.

"It's okay, it's okay, it'll all be okay," Ketelsen told him, sitting on a chair next to him. It was the same room in which Ketelsen had performed the surgery, in which he had seen the frog. In the bed next to his, the convalescing man smiled at him with his uncovered eye, radiant and happy, surrounded by bandages.

"It's understandable, Father," Ketelsen told him. "It happens to a lot of people. These operations cause quite an impression because the patient is only asleep in appearance."

"Is he okay?" asked Lucas, gesturing toward the man who looked like a very peaceful mummy inside his bandages.

"He's doing very well. He woke up without any pain, as we had planned. The one we are worrying about here is you."

The nurse wiped the sweat off his forehead and the awful thought occurred to Lucas that…they were planning to operate on him also. That frog. Might there be one inside him also?

"Are you going to hypnotize me?" he asked, scooting backward on the bed and burying his head into his pillow.

"I wasn't planning on it, but if you want me to I can."

"I'm… I'm not sick," he stammered in a tone of supplication, almost as if he were trying to convince himself of it.

"We hypnotize people who aren't just sick physically. If you would like, we can remove what causes you so much anguish."

His eyes filled with tears and a loathing for his situation swept over him.

"It's just that I can't go on with this... I really can't."

"With what?"

"This doubt."

"Doubt about what?"

"About Him."

"Him?"

"Does He exist?"

"Do you really want to find out?"

"That's all I care about. Imagine my work down in the mission, with this doubt! How can I find out?"

"By dying."

"Of course. But isn't there a less extreme way?"

"I can help you to die."

"That's what I was thinking. From the moment I arrived here I've had that thought. Deep down, you and everyone here... you want to see me in the confession group saying that I am going to die. You're aching to see exactly that happen, aren't you? Did you think I didn't realize that?

"I can help you die and then return. At least if you want to return, of course. Especially if you want to go back *down there*, where you came from."

Lucas asked him a question even though he knew the answer because Susila had told it to him. But he wanted Ketelsen himself to confirm it.

"Can I go back by train?... I can't, can I?"

Ketelsen shook his head gently, no.

"Would I be able to follow the same mountain path I used to get here?"

Ketelsen again shook his head no.

"But didn't you and Susila say that I could go back whenever I wanted?"

"We didn't want to scare you."

"Have you talked to each other about me?"

"Many times."

"And what have you concluded?"

"That we want to help you to return. That we don't understand how you managed to come here. You really don't belong here. Not yet, at least. We realized that from the very beginning. Your utter fear gave it away."

"So do you think that...? Might that be the answer?"

"If you think it is, then it is."

"What risks are involved?"

"It might not work. Or you might wake up here. Or you could wake up in some other place completely different from *here* or *there*."

"How awful! My God!"

"There is always some risk. Especially with tasks like this one."

His entire being stiffened, and he felt a mixture of sensations within him--anxiety, fear, doubt, curiosity, desperation, confidence in Ketelsen, the need to get out of that place once and for all...which really meant removing his soul from its currently convulsed state.

"Fine. Do it. Do it right now."

Ketelsen couldn't hide his satisfaction, mixed with a bit of a morbid glimmer in his huge pupils, it seemed to Lucas.

"Fine, let's get on with it, before you change your mind. With people like you we have to seize the moment to take you to the other side. Put your arms straight down to your sides. Try to relax. Good. Stare at my hand and concentrate on what I am going to say to you. You are actually already in the ideal physical state for hypnosis. All I need to do is transport you back. I need to transport you slightly beyond where you were just now before you awakened. In reality, you may not have even completely returned from there."

"Is this when I say: 'My name is Lucas and I am going to die?'" Lucas was surprised by his humor at that moment.

"Say that when you go to where you are going. You may not need to say it again."

"Very well, then. Goodbye."

"Goodbye. Be benevolent in your report on this place, please. We don't want the *chabochis* to drop in on us... the way you did."

"I promise."

ONCE THE BONDS had been loosed which tied him to the earth, or at least to that spot on the earth, but also to the fatality of a particular given name, to a birth certificate and a particular identity, he felt like he could rise up to the highest parts of the mountains and breath air more fresh than he had ever before breathed (although it was very similar to the air he had been breathing to that point). Perhaps it was the sheer memory of the flavor of air, clear and unpolluted.

Or might it have been (he actually was quite certain) that he had not risen to any part of the mountains and it was simply the effect of the first passes of Ketelsen's magnetic hand--which was like the flapping of a bird's wings--in front of his eyes, back and forth, back and forth, and that was what had separated him from the mountains, the lakes, the faces, his identity.

What is certain is that his ties to everything disappeared, even to his very thoughts, and he ended up in a journey amid crystals and bubbles, like a transparent fish in an infinite shining aquarium.

Didn't he talk about a shining aquarium with the passengers on the train? Do you remember, Lucas? Do you still remember?

Water flowing within water.

A journey through suddenly appearing constellations, through formless, silent symbols.

A kind of smoke undulating within his own personal cocoon. Opening. Closing. Smoke coiling within the smoke.

But within that empty sea, and within that silence which enveloped him, he seemed to have a faint, vague awareness of self.

Lucas Caraveo?

The image of Lucas Caraveo became blurry to him, and it caused him anguish.

All that remained was a dim glow of personal consciousness, but not of a young man or middle-aged man or old man or any kind of man named Lucas, or whatever his name may have been.

Not of things in the present. Not of memories from the past. Not of previews of the future.

It was simply a consciousness not linked to identity, which seemed to be sufficient.

Not places nor time. Nothing.

Just that empty consciousness within that empty, peaceful sea, free from possessions of any kind, completely alone. In a pure time, open and vast.

And this was the marvelous thing that happened at that point: in the silent darkness, in the void free from sensations, something started to become aware of him, to recognize him.

Very vaguely at first, from a vast distance, but little by little the Presence drew near.

It drew nearer and nearer.

The shadow of that new being transformed into brightness and eventually enveloped everything.

Once it was in his consciousness that there was something more than absence and obscurity, his fear and anguish vanished--but not within him, because he was no longer him--and there was an emergent joy, full of peace. As it grew the sensation of peace grew as well, in proportion to the act of being recognized.

It was from being included in that Presence that had been distant but was now approaching him, drawing near to him. In reality it was pure light, a tiny pin of light.

He learned--something which still remained of him learned--that if he continued in that state of joy and drew any closer, he would become lost in that absorbent Presence, and his fear and anguish returned. It returned suddenly and searingly. It was preferable to return to an awareness of his own pain, as insufferable as that was. It hurts, it hurts, he said to himself as he awoke.

He opened his eyes in the mountains, but he could not immediately make out where he was, since something like a dense mist surrounded and embraced him, making it impossible for him to see anything distant. It wasn't an actual mist, but something similar to a mist, because its density veiled his vision, as if volcanic ash were hovering around him.

He took a few steps forward, and then saw the bridge. Darn that Ketelsen--he didn't take into account the bridge. He breathed in, and with all the resolve he could muster placed his foot on the swaying wood. But this time he crossed it quickly--which minimized the swaying, actually--and this time he did not have to deal with even a drop of doubt and he did not hear the beckoning waters beneath. He felt confident that he could return and cross it again.

TWO WEEKS LATER, early in the morning, Lucas saw his superior in the sacristy. Through the open window he could see the kitchen with its tall chimney spitting out tufts of smoke, adjacent to the mission's garden. In the distance, he could see a bluish silhouette of the mountains. Lucas spoke with lowered eyes as he always did in the presence of his superior. His mother was doing better, it was a simple cold that she didn't take care of, and so it deteriorated into acute bronchitis, which is common for someone her age.

"And what about San Sóstenes Valley?" his superior asked, fastening his nearsighted eyes on Lucas like a pair of darts.

"There is no such place, Father. I searched the mountains with a fine-toothed comb, and I can assure you there is no such place."

About the Translator

Timothy Compton is a professor of Spanish at Northern Michigan University. He has studied and published extensively on Mexican theatre, and has published several translations of works by Ignacio Solares and Peruvian writer Ricardo Palma.

LaVergne, TN USA
15 April 2010
179432LV00001B/2/P